Angela and the Broken Heart

Nancy K. Robinson

AN
APPLE
PAPERBACK

SCHOLASTIC INC.
New York Toronto London Auckland Sydney

ISBN 0-590-43211-7

12 11 10 9 8 7 6 5 4 3 2 1   9   1 2 3 4 5 6/9

Printed in the U.S.A.   40

To Amos and my two Sarahs,
for being true to themselves. . . .

List of Chapters

Chapter I

A Visit to Camp

That summer Angela spent two weeks with her parents at the Bluebird Cabins in Maine. Her older brother and sister were working at a summer camp until the end of August.

On the way home Angela and her parents were planning to stop at the camp to visit Tina and Nathaniel.

They had to leave early Sunday morning before the sun came up.

"Nathaniel wants us to come," her mother told her. "Today is Family Day, and he is giving the Sunday service. Children of different religions go to Camp Pinewood, and every Sunday a different counselor or junior counselor is chosen to give the sermon."

"What about Tina?" Angela's father asked. "Does she want us to come, too?"

Angela's mother laughed. "Tina said we could come on one condition: that we pretend not to know her. When I spoke to her on the phone, she said that the little campers in her cabin would no longer respect her if they found out that she had a mother and father. It would interfere with her authority as a counselor-in-training. It would 'destroy her credibility,' she said."

"Sounds like Tina," her father said.

Angela was excited. She had missed her brother and sister. Besides, she was sure Tina would be happy to see *her*.

Angela decided to wear her white shorts, a new black and blue checkered lumber jacket, and her pink and white polka-dot sneakers. She wanted to look her best. She wanted Tina and Nathaniel to be proud to have her as a sister.

No one at Camp Pinewood was wearing a lumber jacket. All the campers were wearing blue shorts and white shirts. Angela stared out the window as they drove past a lake and a volleyball field. She slid down in the backseat so that no one would see what she was wearing.

They drove up to a large building made of dark wooden logs. There was a big sign over the main entrance: WELCOME TO CAMP PINEWOOD, it said. WELCOME TO FAMILY DAY.

Angela would not get out of the car. She pulled the car blanket over her to hide her clothes.

"I'll wait here," she whispered.

"Don't be silly, Angela," her father said.

"Are you going to stay in the car all day?" her mother asked.

Angela nodded. She was six and a half years old and had never felt so out of place in her life.

A girl who looked about thirteen (Tina's age) came over to the car. She was wearing a white shirt and blue shorts, just like everyone else.

"Hi, my name is Nora," she said. She handed Angela's mother a program with a map of the camp. "Sunday services will be held down by the lake. They will begin in ten minutes."

"We'd better hurry," Angela's mother said. "We don't want to be late for Nathaniel's sermon."

Nora gasped and her face turned red. She stared at Angela's mother and father. Then she stuck her head in the window and stared down at Angela.

Angela looked up at the girl who had fuzzy red hair and freckles. She slid down further into the seat.

Suddenly Nora turned and ran over to two girls who were also handing out programs.

Angela pricked up her ears and tried to hear what the girls were saying.

"Can you believe it?" Angela heard Nora whisper. Then she pretended to faint. The other two girls kept looking over at the car. They seemed very excited about something, too.

"I wonder what all that's about," Angela heard her father say.

"I think I have an idea," her mother said.

"Let's go home," Angela whispered.

Now she was sure it wasn't just her lumber jacket. There must be something wrong with everyone in her family.

Her mother got out of the car and held the door open for Angela. Angela refused to budge.

"Is she shy?" Nora was back with the two other

girls, who eagerly introduced themselves.

"I'm Tanya," said one.

"I'm Kate," said the other.

"I don't know what's wrong," Angela's mother said.

"What's her name?"

"This is Angela."

"She's so cute!" Kate squealed.

"We'll take care of her," Nora said. "You go ahead, and we'll bring her down with us."

Nora reached in and tried to lift Angela. Angela shrunk back.

Angela's mother looked puzzled about what to do next. She said, "Well, that's very nice of you, but . . ."

Angela felt like a small animal in a cage at the zoo. She made up her mind in a hurry and slid out from under the blanket. She climbed out of the car.

Her mother sighed with relief. "So you *are* coming with us."

Angela nodded and looked sideways at the three girls. She followed her parents down a path that led to an outdoor chapel in the woods beside the lake.

Her mother said in an undertone, "Tina told me that all the girls at camp are 'in love' with Nathaniel. She said it was 'getting on her nerves.' "

So that was it. Angela felt better. She glanced back at the three girls. She felt a little sorry for them.

Angela sat on a log next to her mother. She looked around. It was beautiful and peaceful under the tall pine trees. She saw her sister Tina seating a group of little campers on a log close to the podium.

Tina was very sunburnt, and her hair was pulled up in a ponytail. She looked healthy, happy, and very serious about her job.

"I guess she has to stay with her group," Angela's mother said.

Angela peeked around. Nora, Tanya, and Kate were sitting on the log right behind Angela and her family.

The service began. Nathaniel stood next to the Reverend Jones, who was the director of the camp. Nathaniel looked very handsome in long white pants, a white shirt, and a blue blazer with a tie.

"Isn't he gorgeous?" Tanya whispered.

Angela agreed. Nathaniel's hair was longer than usual and curled around his collar.

The Reverend Jones welcomed the parents to Family Day and said he wanted to tell them a little history of Camp Pinewood.

"Ten years ago," Nora whispered.

"Ten years ago," the Reverend Jones began in a deep voice.

". . . my wife and I stopped off . . ." Nora went on.

". . . my wife and I stopped off for a picnic in the woods on the way to visit some relatives. . . ."

Tanya and Kate were giggling. Angela had a feeling that it was not the first time the Reverend Jones had told this story.

"We were walking . . ." the Reverend Jones went on.

". . . down this very path . . ." Nora whispered.

". . . down this very path. We looked at the tall pines; we looked at the wood. . . ."

"We turned to one another . . ." Nora went on.

"We turned to one another and said, 'This place could never be called anything but Pinewood. Wouldn't it be nice if we could gather together children of every different faith. . . .' "

The Reverend Jones went on and on. Angela watched Nathaniel. He didn't seem nervous. But Angela's heart was pounding.

Finally, the Reverend Jones introduced Nathaniel as "a very special young man who has contributed so much to the spirit of Camp Pinewood in such a short time."

Nora sighed loudly. Then the three girls were quiet.

Nathaniel opened the Bible he was holding and placed it on the wooden stand in front of him. He reached into his blazer pocket, took out a pair of eyeglasses, cleaned them with a handkerchief, and then set them on his nose. He glanced down at the text briefly.

Angela was very impressed.

Nathaniel looked up and studied the audience for a long time. Finally he began:

Chapter II

A Bible Story

"I'm sure you all remember the story from the Bible about Noah and the ark . . . how Noah collected two of every animal on the face of the earth . . . how it rained for forty days and forty nights."

Nathaniel was a good speaker and in no time at all he had the full attention of the parents and campers. The Reverend Jones stood by, smiling and nodding. His eyes seemed glazed over. Angela was not sure he was really listening to Nathaniel.

Nathaniel cleared his throat and glanced down at the text again.

" . . . And so it came to pass that on the thirtieth

day, the animals in the ark became restless. They were bored, they wanted to be entertained. The larger animals — the elephants, the rhinos, and the hippopotamuses — began picking on the smaller ones. They threatened to go on the rampage."

Angela heard Nora mutter, "He's talking about Bunk Nine. Remember how they went wild the week it rained and they had pillow fights and raided the other cabins?"

"Noah tried to reason with them, but to no avail," Nathaniel went on. "Suddenly the sky turned dark. A bolt of lightning flashed across the heavens. . . ."

Angela felt her mother stiffen. She looked up. Her mother's face was pale. Her eyes were wide open.

Angela was surprised that her mother was so frightened by a Bible story. Angela wasn't frightened. She was enjoying the story. And so, it seemed, was everyone else in the camp.

There was a hush as Nathaniel described how "out of the blackness of the deep a wave rose up and hit the ark. The animals big and small got the message:

". . . that we're all in the same boat," Nathaniel concluded. Nathaniel went on to explain how important cooperation was — "between children big and small." And how important it was to take part in rainy-day games "in a cheerful way, without grumbling and complaining."

"He *is* talking about Bunk Nine," Nora whispered.

Everyone was very impressed with Nathaniel's sermon. After the service people came up to him and shook his hand. The Reverend Jones told everyone it was one of the finest sermons ever given at Camp Pinewood, "and I believe Nathaniel's message is clear to each and every one of us."

Angela was bursting with pride.

But her mother still seemed very shaken. Angela saw her take Nathaniel aside. They seemed to be arguing about something. But just then Nathaniel spotted Angela and scooped her up in his arms. He introduced her to everyone.

Angela had a wonderful afternoon. Tina gave her a tour of her cabin. (Tina was very nice to Angela, but she introduced her mother and father as "Angela's parents.")

They had box lunches on a big lawn. Later that afternoon everyone went for a swim.

Nathaniel's best friend Doug was a lifeguard at the waterfront. He was the one who noticed that Angela had learned to swim that summer in Maine.

"She does an excellent dog paddle," Doug told her parents.

Then Tina took Angela on a "private" walk through the woods and told her a secret. "I have to tell somebody."

Tina took a deep breath.

"Everyone in camp has been telling me all summer that Doug likes me, even though Doug hasn't actually said anything."

Angela was very happy for Tina. Tina had always liked Nathaniel's best friend.

"One night," Tina spoke in a whisper, "all the counselors and junior counselors went on a hayride in the moonlight. I was sitting next to Doug and I think he wanted to kiss me, but I got a piece of hay in my mouth and it cut my lip and I had to go to the infirmary."

Tina looked down at her little sister. "Do you

think he would have kissed me if that hadn't happened?"

"Oh, yes!" Angela said with great confidence.

"Are you sure?" Tina asked.

"Positive," Angela said.

"That's what I wrote in my letter to Melissa. You see, I got a letter from her. She met this boy at a dance at her camp. His name is Rutherford, but she calls him 'Rocky dear.' She's in love. She said it's really serious, but she only danced with him once. Don't you think it sounds a little superficial compared to me and Doug?"

"Yes," Angela said.

Angela was delighted that her older sister was asking her opinion on such a grown-up subject.

There was a campfire that evening. Nathaniel performed his Great Waldo the Magician act, a magic act where everything goes wrong — the rabbit keeps appearing instead of disappearing while the magician tries to cover up his failures. Angela had seen it many times before, but everyone was laughing so hard, she had to laugh, too. It was an exciting day. By the end of it Angela was exhausted.

On the drive home Angela's father went on and on about Nathaniel and how grown up he had become in such a short time. "I never knew he was such an athlete. Did you see him dive? And that *sermon*."

Angela's mother didn't say anything. She was unusually quiet.

"Is something the matter?" her father finally asked her mother.

Her mother burst out, "Well, I would have thought that you would have noticed, too."

"Noticed what?"

"That Nathaniel made up that story. It's not in the Bible."

"Of course the story of Noah's ark is in the Bible," her father said.

"Not the way Nathaniel told it," her mother snapped. "The animals in the ark never got restless."

"But he had a Bible right in front of him." Angela's father was quiet for a moment. After a while he said, "Well, it certainly sounded real. 'Out of the blackness of the deep' and all that."

"He made it up," her mother said in a flat voice.

"Well, it certainly was entertaining. And

Nathaniel made his point very well."

Angela's mother was shocked. "How can you say such a thing? I can't believe his nerve. He said he didn't have much time to prepare the sermon, so he just made it up."

Her father was quiet for a few minutes, but Angela noticed he was making a funny sniffing sound as he drove.

Angela's mother turned and glared at her husband. "Are you laughing? How could you? It's not the least bit funny."

"Reverend Jones didn't even notice." Angela's father *was* laughing. "I have a feeling he wasn't really listening anyway. If you ask me, Jessica, our son did a wonderful job. Did you notice the way he took off his eyeglasses and used them to emphasize a point?"

"Darling," Jessica Steele said in her coldest voice, "our son does not wear eyeglasses."

"That's true," Angela's father said thoughtfully. "I wonder where he got them."

Angela gasped. The eyeglasses fit in so well. Angela had not even questioned them.

Her parents argued all the way back to the city.

"Well, if you ask *me*, Nathaniel is getting a little

too sure of himself," her mother was saying. "He's getting too big for his britches. He's becoming arrogant. There's no way to punish him, I guess, but if he doesn't watch out, he'll get his comeuppance."

Angela had never heard that word before. She sounded it out. "Come-up-pince."

She had no idea what it meant, but it scared her. She loved her brother. She wanted him to be happy and sure of himself all the time. She didn't want him to get any comeuppance.

But she felt extremely uncomfortable about what Nathaniel had done. She didn't think you were supposed to make up Bible stories . . .

. . . and she knew for certain that it was very wrong to pretend to wear eyeglasses!

"It might even be against the law," she told herself.

Chapter III

Meet Moxie

Angela worried about Nathaniel all that night. When they got back to their apartment in the city, there was a storm.

Angela lay in her bed and hoped that it wasn't thundering and lightning at Camp Pinewood. She didn't want Nathaniel struck by a bolt of lightning. Sho didn't want a big wave to rise "out of the blackness of the deep" of Pinewood Lake and flood the entire camp as a punishment to Nathaniel. . . . Angela couldn't seem to stop these terrible thoughts.

Angela decided to put herself to sleep by counting sheep.

Angela never counted sheep jumping over fences. She felt it was too dangerous. She was afraid one of the little lambs might break a leg. So Angela counted sheep jumping rope. But tonight, to Angela's horror, all the sheep were wearing eyeglasses just like Nathaniel's.

Angela finally put herself to sleep by repeating the word comeuppance over and over again.

The word comeuppance did not seem to be in Angela's little dictionary. She spent some time early Monday morning trying to figure out how to get the big dictionary down from the bookshelf in the living room. It was up too high. It was too heavy. Her parents were still asleep. She didn't want to ask them anyway. She didn't want her mother to get angry at Nathaniel all over again.

At nine o'clock the doorbell rang. Madeline, a girl who lived on the first floor, was standing outside in the hallway trembling.

"I'm so glad you're back!" she said when Angela opened the door. "Tony and Pamela have been away for two weeks, and Moxie is giving me looks!"

Moxie was a young black cat who lived in the building. Her owners went away often, and

Madeline, who was eleven years old, had the job of feeding Moxie.

But Madeline was afraid of Moxie, so she paid Angela twenty-five cents a weekend to hold her hand when she entered the apartment, locate Moxie so that Moxie wouldn't jump out and scare her, and to "entertain" Moxie.

Entertaining Moxie consisted of petting her, talking to her, and playing games that a cat would enjoy. Madeline called it Moxie's "quality time."

"You won't believe what she did while you were away," Madeline went on. "She pulled out a whole roll of toilet paper. It's all over the place. She never would have done that if you had been here. Moxie always behaves when you are around."

Moxie seemed happy to see Angela. She rubbed up against Angela's leg. She purred and then stood looking up at Angela as if expecting some explanation of Angela's absence.

Madeline stayed as far away from Moxie as she could. She went to open a can of cat food.

Angela took out Moxie's basket of toys. Moxie had a lot of toys. "That's because Tony and Pamela have guilty complexes for leaving her alone so much," was Madeline's explanation.

Angela let Moxie pick the toy she wanted to play with. Moxie picked a black furry mouse as black as Moxie herself.

Right before Angela left for Maine she had given Moxie a lesson in fetching, but Moxie usually just watched the mouse and then looked at Angela.

But today Moxie leaped after the mouse and brought it back to Angela in her teeth. Angela was amazed. Angela threw it again. Moxie fetched it.

"Madeline!" Angela called. "Moxie can fetch!"

Madeline stood on the other side of the living room and watched. She was very impressed.

"You're extremely good with cats," Madeline said.

Angela knew that. She had never told anyone, but when she grew up, she planned to have a school for cats. She thought about it a lot. She even drew maps of the school and worked on lesson plans.

"Don't ever go away on vacation again," Madeline said. "Moxie was getting psy-cat-trick problems."

While Madeline went to change the kitty litter

and roll up the toilet paper, Angela curled up in the easy chair and got ready to read to Moxie.

Angela was a good reader, and Moxie enjoyed being read to. Tony and Pamela had a lovely edition of *Grimms' Fairy Tales*. Angela opened the book to the first story. She had promised Moxie she would read "The Twelve Dancing Princesses" as soon as she got back from Maine.

Moxie jumped up onto the arm of the easy chair, curled up against Angela's shoulder, closed her eyes, and waited for Angela to begin:

" 'THE TWELVE DANCING PRINCESSES

" 'Once upon a time there was a king who had twelve daughters, each more beautiful than the other. They slept together in a hall where their beds stood close to one another. At night when they had gone to bed, the King locked the door and bolted it. But when he unlocked it in the morning, he noticed that their shoes had been danced to pieces, and nobody could explain how it happened.' "

Moxie brushed her whiskers against Angela's cheek and began to purr.

" 'So the King sent out a proclamation saying that anyone who could discover where the princesses did their night's dancing might choose one of them to be his wife, and should reign after his death. But whoever presented himself, and failed to make the discovery after three days and nights, was to forfeit his life.' "

"That means he gets his head chopped off," Angela explained to Moxie.

Moxie stared at Angela, but she didn't seem frightened, so Angela went on.

Madeline came and sat quietly on the couch and listened. When Angela had finished the story, Madeline said, "Angela, I am going to visit my grandparents in Florida over Valentine's Day weekend, and I was wondering if you could take care of Moxie while I am away."

"Take care of Moxie all by myself?" Angela asked. "But I'm only six and a half." She thought a moment. "Wait a minute. My birthday is the day before Valentine's Day. It's February thirteenth."

"You see!" Madeline said. "You'll be seven years old. You will have six months to grow some maturity."

Angela looked at Madeline. Madeline was always using big words. Maybe she knew what it meant to get a comeuppance.

"Do you know what a comeuppance is?" she asked.

"Use it in a sentence," Madeline said sharply.

Angela did her best to remember exactly what her mother had said in the car. "If he doesn't watch out, he'll get his comeuppance."

"Who?" Madeline wanted to know.

"Somebody," Angela whispered.

"Come-up-pince." Madeline sounded it out. "Are you sure it isn't come-up-pinch?"

Angela was pretty sure it wasn't, but she said, "What does *that* mean?"

"I don't know," Madeline said, "but I'll bet I can work it out." She got a piece of paper from the telephone table and began to write. "You see," she explained to Angela, "every word has a square root."

Angela watched her. She was impressed with

the squiggles and lines Madeline was making on the paper.

But finally Madeline gave up. "I'll find out for you," she told Angela. "I don't think it's a word exactly; I think it might be an *expression*."

Angela went down with Madeline to her apartment. "Are you going to look it up in a dictionary?" Angela asked.

"No," Madeline said. "I'm going to ask my mother."

"I'll wait outside," Angela said in a small voice.

Angela waited in the hall. Finally Madeline came to the door. "I found out," she said. "My mother says it's a very old-fashioned expression."

"What does it mean?"

"It means 'splat,' " Madeline told her.

"Splat?" Angela asked.

Madeline explained that if you went around thinking you were the greatest thing in the world, something would happen and then "splat."

"Like Humpty Dumpty," she said.

Chapter IV

The Real Nathaniel

Two weeks later Tina and Nathaniel returned home from camp. Angela was relieved to see that Nathaniel was all right. In fact, he seemed to be on top of the world.

Nathaniel's suitcase was filled with letters from campers. "Love letters," Tina said. "Letters from his fans."

Angela noticed that he had not even opened some of them.

"Are you going to answer them?" Angela was painfully aware that some of the girls who had written to him had used their best stationery and stickers.

One envelope had two big red lipstick kisses over the back flap. SEALED WITH A KISS, it said. It had Nora's return address on it.

"Are you going to write back to Nora?" Angela asked.

"Are you kidding?" Nathaniel laughed. "Write back to her? I have better things to do with my time."

His laugh reminded Angela of some old cartoons she had seen at her friend Mandy's birthday party. Whenever any cartoon character laughed like that, he either stepped off a cliff the next moment, or got flattened by a boulder.

"Please don't laugh that way," Angela begged her brother. But Nathaniel didn't seem to hear her. He laughed another heartless laugh.

The real Nathaniel never laughed that way. Angela was beginning to wonder if her brother had returned from camp a different person.

Nathaniel was starting high school. He was going into tenth grade. It was a big high school. The night before school started he seemed a little nervous.

"You see," he told his family at dinner, "this is the big time. You've got to make an impression the first day. You have to make sure people notice you. Otherwise, you're just another kid — a nobody."

Angela was going into second grade and wasn't the least bit worried. In fact, she was looking forward to seeing all her classmates, but especially Eddie Bishop.

Eddie had been her friend since kindergarten. There was only one thing that made her a little nervous. She had told Eddie that as soon as the summer was over, she would let him know if she were going to marry him.

"What are you going to wear tomorrow?" she heard Tina ask Nathaniel.

"I'm not sure," Nathaniel said. "I guess I'm just going to be myself."

"Sounds very sensible," Angela heard her mother murmur approvingly.

Everyone was quiet at breakfast the next morning. Angela was sure they were trying not to look at Nathaniel. Angela's father kept clearing his throat as if he were about to say something to Nathaniel. But then he seemed to think better of it.

Nathaniel's hair was slicked back on both sides. The hair on the top of his head was standing stiffly up straight except for a spit curl that fell over his forehead.

He had never worn his hair like that before. His clothes were different, too. Nathaniel was wearing blue jeans with holes in the knees, and a black T-shirt with white lettering that said, UP AGAINST THE WALL, LITTERBUGS.

Nathaniel had nicked himself shaving and he had little pieces of tissue all over his face to stop the blood. Nathaniel had never shaved before. He didn't need to shave. He had no hair on his face. There was a heavy smell of after-shave lotion at the breakfast table.

Suddenly Nathaniel pushed his plate away and said, "You don't have to say it. I know what you're all thinking and you're wrong."

Angela had a feeling she had missed something. What was everyone thinking that made Nathaniel so mad? Or what did Nathaniel think everyone was thinking that made him so mad? Or maybe it was what did everyone think Nathaniel was thinking they were thinking. . . .

Her mother said, "Well, I was just wondering about those jeans. . . ."

Nathaniel exploded. "Why do you always have to criticize me? Why can't you just let me be myself?"

No one said anything for a while.

"What time is Doug coming to pick you up?" Tina finally asked Nathaniel.

"I'm not walking to school with Doug," Nathaniel said.

Tina was shocked. "You're not?"

Nathaniel shook his head. "I'm not sure I want to be seen hanging out with him the first day. I've got to meet new people."

"Does that mean Doug isn't coming here after school?" Tina asked.

Ever since third grade Doug and Nathaniel had been best friends. They were both interested in science. They always worked together on science projects. Doug was always around the house.

"You know, Tina," Nathaniel said, "not everyone considers Doug the coolest kid in the world."

Tina gasped and stared at Nathaniel. "And I suppose you think you're cool."

Nathaniel shrugged.

Tina wailed. "Now what am I going to do?"

"About what?" Nathaniel asked crossly.

"Nothing," Tina mumbled.

The doorbell rang. Tina jumped up to answer it. She was back a moment later. She had a strange look on her face.

"Nathaniel!" Tina said. "Doug says he doesn't mind walking Angela to school with you. What does he mean by that? *I'm* the one who walks her to school."

Nathaniel looked very upset.

"Is that what you told Doug?" his mother whispered. "That you couldn't go with him because you were taking Angela to school?"

Nathaniel nodded. "Yes, but I'm not really taking Angela to school. I only said that . . ."

"It's okay with me," Tina said quickly. "I've taken Angela to school ever since she was in kindergarten. I guess it's your turn. You can pick her up, too."

"What a good idea," their mother said. "This year Nathaniel will take Angela to school and bring her home. It only seems fair."

"But I can't," Nathaniel said desperately. "I'll be late myself."

"No, you won't," his mother said. "Not if you leave soon."

Nathaniel turned to Tina and whispered, "Does Doug have the top button of his shirt buttoned?"

Tina nodded. "He looks nice."

Nathaniel groaned. "Look, I'll take Angela to school, but I don't want to be seen with Doug." He paused. "Tina, tell Doug something — anything!"

Tina thought for a moment. "Maybe I'll say that Angela is a little scared about the first day of school and it might be better if . . ."

"That's good," Nathaniel said. "Tell him that."

Tina left the kitchen.

" 'Oh, what a tangled web we weave,' " their father began, " 'when first we practice to deceive.' "

"What makes you say that?" Nathaniel asked.

"*I* didn't say it. Sir Walter Scott said it," his father said.

"Well, what's it supposed to mean?" Nathaniel grumbled.

"Figure it out for yourself," their father said.

Nathaniel sighed. "Well, I'm telling the truth now because I *am* taking Angela to school. . . ."

". . . And I *am* a little scared," Angela said in a whisper.

Nathaniel gave his little sister a grateful look.

Angela *was* feeling a little scared. Not about the first day of school. It had suddenly occurred to her that Eddie might have completely forgotten that Angela was supposed to let him know today if she was going to marry him.

What if Eddie didn't say anything at all? It would be embarrassing to have to remind him.

Suddenly Angela had a plan.

First she would ask Eddie if he liked cats. (Angela had no intention of giving up her career as the headmistress of a school for cats.) If he said "yes," Angela would say, "Well, then the answer is 'yes.' "

If Eddie looked puzzled, she would change the subject.

Angela sat up straight and looked her brother up and down. For years she had wanted Eddie Bishop and her brother Nathaniel to meet each other.

"Nathaniel," she said, "if you're taking me to school, you'll have to wear something else."

Her father laughed out loud. Her mother's eyes were twinkling.

"What's wrong with what I'm wearing?" Nathaniel growled.

Angela took a deep breath. "Well, your T-shirt is nice, but you'll have to wear pants without holes. Even Eddie, who is very *very* poor, has patches to cover the holes in his pants. And . . . um . . . your head comes to a point when you wear your hair like that."

"Maybe I should wear a suit and a tie," Nathaniel said.

"That would be nice," Angela said. "Yes," she said happily. "That's just what you should wear."

Chapter V

A Proposal of Marriage

Three months had passed since the day Cheryl White had followed Angela and Eddie around the schoolyard chanting, "Angela's going to marry Eddie. Angela's going to marry Eddie."

"Maybe I am," Angela finally said, but only to shut Cheryl up.

Cheryl grabbed Angela, took her aside, and said, "If you marry Eddie, you'll be poor. You'll have to live over there in that broken-down house with Eddie's grandmother and all of his brothers and sisters. Your pajamas will be hanging on that clothesline, too. You'll never get to eat out in a restaurant."

Angela looked at the run-down buildings in the lot behind the school. She thought it was unfair that everyone could see how poor Eddie was, right from the school playground.

Angela shrugged and said, "I don't care."

Cheryl ran and told Eddie that Angela wanted to marry him.

Eddie shrugged, too. "I already know I'm going to marry Angela," he said. When he saw Angela had heard, he looked embarrassed. Later on he said, "You don't have to marry me if you don't want to. You can let me know later. You can let me know in second grade."

"I'll let you know the first day of school," Angela promised.

A week later at the class picnic, Angela got a little worried when she saw her friend Mandy chasing Eddie around. She was sorry she hadn't said "yes" right away.

"Where's Angela?" Melissa was waiting for Tina at the corner. "Aren't we taking her to school?"

"Nathaniel's taking her to school this year," Tina said.

Melissa and Tina walked to school together

every day. For years Melissa Glenn had treated Angela like a package that had to be dropped off.

"Well," Melissa said, "it's a good thing Angela's *not* here. I have to talk to you, Tina. You won't believe what's going on. My mother is trying to break up my relationship with Rocky!"

Melissa pushed up the sleeve of her light pink cashmere sweater. Her silver bracelet sparkled in the sunlight. She called it her "Going Steady Bracelet." The name ROCKY was engraved on it.

Tina was the only one who knew that Melissa had bought the bracelet herself. She had ordered it from her mother's jewelry store as soon as she returned from camp. "Rocky would want me to have it," she said.

"What is your mother doing?" Tina asked. "How is she trying to break you and Rocky up?"

Tina wondered why her life never seemed as dramatic as Melissa's.

"She's forcing me to take ballroom dancing lessons at the Tudor Classes. You're taking them, too, Tina."

"I am?" Tina asked.

"Yes," Melissa said. "My mother is calling your

mother tonight. Nathaniel has to come, too."

Tina was surprised that Melissa was still interested in Nathaniel now that she was supposed to be madly in love with Rocky.

Melissa flashed her bracelet at Tina again.

"By the way," Melissa said. "How is your love life? How's Doug?"

"Oh, fine," Tina said.

"Ouch, Nathaniel," Angela whispered. "You're squishing my hand."

Nathaniel hadn't realized he was holding his little sister's hand so tightly. He had butterflies in his stomach. He didn't want to go to high school. He wished he were back in second grade.

He looked around at the small children who were running around the elementary school playground, laughing and calling to each other.

"Not a care in the world," he thought. Little did they know what lay before them. Little did they know what it meant to have serious things to think about — important things.

"Does my head really look pointy?" he asked Angela.

Angela studied him. "It doesn't look *so* pointy," she said. "It looks okay. You look like that rock star. . . ."

"What rock star?" Nathaniel asked.

"I forget his name," Angela said. "He's kind of funny-looking."

Nathaniel felt a little better. Any rock star was all right with him.

Angela had seemed a little disappointed that he wasn't wearing a suit, but Nathaniel had changed his jeans. He was wearing jeans without holes, but he had tucked a pair of scissors into his book bag, just in case everyone at high school had holes in their jeans. He would cut them up secretly — maybe in the bathroom.

"Why, Nathaniel, I almost didn't recognize you!"

Nathaniel looked down at Miss Berry. Miss Berry had been his kindergarten teacher.

"You look terrific," Miss Berry said. She grinned. "And I love your T-shirt. I could use a T-shirt like that. Nothing annoys me more than people dropping things on the ground."

"I had the same problem myself when I was

working at this summer camp. . . ." Nathaniel began.

It was hard to believe that his kindergarten teacher was talking to him as an equal. Maybe he *was* ready for high school.

Angela was looking up at them both with shining eyes.

Miss Berry had to excuse herself. Suddenly, once again, Nathaniel was overcome with a horrible dread. He took Angela's hand again.

"Are we waiting for Eddie?" he asked.

Angela nodded.

"I can't wait much longer," Nathaniel said. "I'll be late for school."

"Maybe you can take a bus," Angela said.

Nathaniel sighed. "I'd rather walk. I guess I'll have to meet Eddie Bishop tomorrow."

"Just one more minute," Angela begged him. She scanned the playground for her friend. Suddenly she pulled her hand away and started to run.

Angela was running across the playground. She was running so fast she seemed to be flying. Nathaniel followed her, expecting to see her meet

Eddie, but instead she joined a bunch of little kids who were gathered around the school fence. They were watching a bulldozer in the lot behind the school.

Across the street the lot was now empty except for a big hole in the ground. Nathaniel had trouble remembering what had been there before. He vaguely remembered some shabby buildings with tar paper roofs.

Nathaniel looked down at his little sister. Angela seemed fascinated by the construction site. When Nathaniel told her he had to leave, she didn't turn around. She seemed to have forgotten all about introducing him to Eddie Bishop. She never even turned around to say, "Good-bye."

Nathaniel left for school wishing that he were still young enough to find bulldozers and power drills interesting.

The high school was twelve blocks away. Nathaniel checked his reflection in store windows, car mirrors, and shiny public telephone boxes. He wished he had brought a mirror in his book bag, but he had a horrible picture of everything falling out of his book bag, and someone discovering he had brought a mirror to school!

The steps were crowded with students. Nathaniel stopped short and put on his windbreaker. He zipped it up. He was glad he had brought it with him. No one seemed to be wearing T-shirts with messages printed on them.

Nathaniel climbed the steps. There were clusters of students talking together, but he didn't see anyone from his junior high school.

It was five minutes to nine. Nathaniel stood alone on the steps looking at his watch, as if he were expecting to meet someone.

At three minutes to nine he began searching the crowd for Doug, but all he saw was a sea of unfamiliar faces.

By the time the bell rang, Nathaniel felt desperate. Where was Doug? He finally turned and started up the steps. He felt a poke in his back.

He whirled around. "Doug!" he said.

But it wasn't Doug. A girl was poking him with

her cello case. She didn't even notice, she was so busy talking to two of her friends.

She poked him again.

"Sorry." Nathaniel apologized to the cello case, and felt even more foolish.

Chapter VI

Keeping Bisy

No one seemed to know what had happened to Eddie Bishop. Miss Berry, the kindergarten teacher, didn't know. Miss Mason, who had been Angela's first-grade teacher, didn't know either. "I'll see if I can find out," she told Angela gently.

The only other child who seemed to care was Cheryl White. Angela was surprised. Cheryl had always hated Eddie.

"Maybe they're in the poorhouse," Cheryl suggested. "I'll bet they are in the poorhouse."

Angela was sure Cheryl was wrong.

A little while later, Cheryl said, "Maybe his house blew away, like in The Wizard of Oz."

Angela had not read *The Wizard of Oz*. She had not seen the movie. She did not know what Cheryl was talking about.

Angela kept her eye on the door of her classroom. She was sure Eddie's family had not moved too far away. Any minute now Eddie would walk in.

Her second-grade teacher's name was Miss Blizzard. She was the largest woman Angela had ever seen. She wasn't fat, just tall and broad-shouldered. She wore a loose gray suit, and big, heavy, brown shoes. She had a sharp no-nonsense voice. When Miss Blizzard called the class to attention, no one wiggled around in their seats.

"Eddie would wiggle if he were here," Angela thought.

Cheryl White was sitting behind Angela. There was an empty seat in front of Angela.

"Are you saving that seat for Eddie?" Cheryl wanted to know.

Angela shrugged. "He can sit there if he wants to," she murmured.

"What if Eddie doesn't come?"

Angela pretended not to hear Cheryl's question.

Cheryl kept poking her and repeating the question. "What if Eddie doesn't come?"

Finally Angela wrote a note to Cheryl.

I AM BISY, it said. She turned and put it on Cheryl's desk.

Suddenly the door of the classroom swung open. Angela turned her head quickly and looked out the window. It was a warm September day, but Angela's face suddenly felt so hot she was sure she was running a fever.

She held her breath and prayed that Eddie would take the seat right in front of her.

"You're late," Angela heard Miss Blizzard say. "Don't let it happen again. Take the seat over there."

Angela heard a loud clatter in front of her and turned to see what was going on. A boy she had never seen before was trying to get into the desk in front of her, but he was very clumsy. He had knocked over the chair.

"Now what?" Miss Blizzard said. The boy gave the teacher a dazed look and stared at the chair on the floor.

Angela stood up and picked up the chair. She

did not want to help the new boy. She did not want him to sit in Eddie's seat, but he seemed so confused.

The new boy was skinny. He was wearing jeans and a blue and white striped shirt. He sat down without looking at Angela and stared down at his desk.

Miss Blizzard took out her seating chart and asked everyone to stand up and say their name in a "nice clear voice." They went around the room. When it was the new boy's turn, he got up and stood there, looking at the floor. He seemed unable to speak.

"Well?" Miss Blizzard said.

The boy shifted his gaze to a map on the wall.

"Just say your name," Cheryl whispered impatiently. Then she waved her hand. "He doesn't know what to do," she told Miss Blizzard. "He wasn't in our school last year."

"Well, then, perhaps you should tell the class a little about yourself," Miss Blizzard said.

The boy was silent.

Suddenly Angela noticed something. On the back pocket of the boy's jeans was a leather patch. On the patch was the boy's name. LEE, it said.

Angela felt very clever. She was sure she was the only one in the class who knew his name. She wondered if she should raise her hand and introduce him to the class. She would say, "This is Lee."

Miss Blizzard was studying the new boy. "Well, maybe you'll feel a little more comfortable later." Her voice wasn't as sharp as before. "Have a seat. Next," she called.

Angela stood up and said her name in a nice clear voice.

Miss Blizzard said that she was going to give homework every night. "I expect everyone to work hard in this class. We have a lot to cover," she said. She passed out the worksheets and books. Angela was happy. She wanted to keep busy. She wrote the math assignment down twice — once for her and once for Eddie. She would help Eddie catch up as soon as he arrived.

Later that morning the second-grade class went to the school library to choose books.

"Every day we will have silent reading," Miss Blizzard explained. "I will expect a book report from each of you as soon as you have finished the book you have chosen."

When Angela's turn came to choose a book, she chose *The Wizard of Oz*.

"Isn't that a little hard for you?" the librarian asked.

Angela shook her head. She liked sounding out new words. "I want to read it," she said.

Miss Blizzard nodded. "A child should have a challenge," she said.

Angela took the book back to her classroom and opened it. "This book is dedicated to my good friend and comrade, my wife L.F.B. . . ."

Angela felt a tugging at her heart. She missed Eddie very much right at that minute.

She turned the page quickly. There was a list of chapters, a map of the land of Oz, but on page one there was a different book. It was called *The Cyclone*.

Angela turned the page and breathed a sigh of relief. At the top of page two, on the left side, it said *The Wizard of Oz* again.

"When Dorothy stood in the doorway
and looked around she could see nothing
but the great gray prairie . . ."

"There must be two books in one," she thought.

Angela began to struggle through the beginning, carefully reading only the pages on the left that said *The Wizard of Oz*. She ignored the other book called *The Cyclone* that appeared on the right-hand pages.

On the way to lunch Angela noticed that the new boy was standing alone outside the door of the lunchroom. He seemed afraid to go in.

"What's his problem?" Cheryl asked and giggled.

Suddenly Angela felt very sorry for the new boy. She went over to him.

"Hello, Lee," she whispered.

But he didn't turn around. "Hello, Lee," she said in a louder voice. He turned around and looked at her in surprise.

Angela wanted him to feel at home, so she said, "Um, Lee, I should warn you to stay away from the egg salad sandwiches. Those are the ones in the blue-and-white wrappers. Sometimes there are pieces of shells in them."

The boy suddenly smiled at her. "Really?" he asked.

Lee followed Angela into the cafeteria. She introduced him to Cheryl and Mandy. He seemed very grateful to Angela for all her advice about the food. He sat with Angela and her friends. "This is Lee," Angela said to everyone who came to sit at the table, and Lee said, "Hi."

Lee went to dump his tray.

"How did you know his name?" Mandy wanted to know.

Angela felt very smart. "It's written on the back of his pants." She pointed. "Look, it says LEE."

Cheryl gasped. "Angela, his name isn't Lee. LEE is the name of the blue jean company."

"That's right," Mandy said.

Right after lunch Miss Blizzard introduced the new boy. His name was Luther.

Angela was so embarrassed, she spent the rest of the day ignoring him. He kept turning around to look at her, but she pretended not to notice. He followed her around the classroom, but she avoided him. What if Eddie walked in and thought she had a new boyfriend?

Angela was beginning to dislike the new boy

very much. She disliked him for sitting in Eddie's seat. She disliked him for making a fool of her by letting her call him Lee.

"I'll never think I know anything again," she told herself. "Never in my whole life."

Chapter VII

The Beautiful Lola

The girl with the cello case was in Nathaniel's homeroom. Her name was Lola Mendes.

Every time Nathaniel walked through a doorway, she was right behind him, poking him with her cello case.

She poked him again as they were leaving the homeroom. He turned around.

Nathaniel felt like saying something like: "You might be interested to know that my father plays the cello, too — but he's a professional. He doesn't go around poking people with his case."

Nathaniel's father made his living playing the cello in the city orchestra.

Nathaniel glared at Lola, but she was busy talking to her girlfriends. He couldn't tell if she was poking him on purpose.

Lola muttered something to her friend Pat. Pat kept looking over at Nathaniel.

The other girl was short with a long whitish-blonde ponytail. Her name was Grace.

Grace whispered something to Lola. Lola laughed.

"Snorted," Nathaniel told himself. "That girl has a laugh like a horse."

Nathaniel was beginning to suspect that Lola was talking about him — that she was laughing at him.

Was it his T-shirt that said UP AGAINST THE WALL, LITTERBUGS? Quickly Nathaniel zipped up his windbreaker.

He decided to stop in the bathroom and check out the way he looked.

"My hair looks ridiculous," he thought. He wet it and tried to get rid of the spit curl on his forehead. Then he dried his hair with a paper towel. He stared into the mirror. His hair looked even worse.

Nathaniel looked at his program card. His next

class was biology in Room 402. If he didn't leave right now, he would be late.

Nathaniel walked into biology class just as the second bell rang. He took a seat in the last row.

His heart stood still. Lola was in his biology class, too.

He looked around for Doug. For years Nathaniel and Doug had been talking about becoming lab partners in high school biology. Together they would make breakthroughs in the frontiers of science and medicine.

But Doug wasn't in his biology class. Nathaniel felt lost without Doug.

He found himself staring at Lola, watching everything she did. She opened her notebook and began taking notes. Her mouth twitched as she wrote. On the third finger of her right hand she wore a silver ring with a large delicate butterfly on it.

She caught him looking at her and studied him for a few seconds without a flicker of interest.

"As if I were an insect," Nathaniel thought, and he tried not to look at her again.

But he couldn't help himself. Lola was wearing

a white blouse and an emerald-green hockey tunic with a charcoal-gray skirt over it. She had black lace-up hockey boots and thick cotton socks. She didn't wear any lipstick or makeup.

"She probably thinks she's so beautiful, she doesn't need any," he thought.

She had thick dark hair, long eyelashes, and a smooth tan complexion. Her big dark eyes drooped down at the corners. She wore no jewelry other than the silver butterfly ring.

In between classes, Nathaniel saw Doug at the bottom of the staircase. Doug was talking to a boy Nathaniel recognized. Neil had been in the class ahead of them in junior high school. He had been very popular and was considered "cool."

Nathaniel could not get down the stairs fast enough. By the time he reached the bottom, Doug was gone.

Right before lunch Nathaniel had gym class. He changed into his shorts and shirt and went outside for track and field.

As he was passing the hockey field he saw Lola playing field hockey. Lola played right inner. She was running very fast and carrying the ball. Lola passed it to her friend Pat, her right wing.

Pat dribbled the ball down the alley and scored a goal.

Nathaniel stood still and watched.

The center forward was now standing in the circle on the forward line waiting for the referee to put the ball into play. Lola put her stick on the ground in waiting position for the next play.

The center forward won the face-off and passed the ball to Lola. Nathaniel moved closer and watched in amazement as Lola zigzagged down the field dribbling the ball.

Suddenly the other team's fullback moved in front of Lola and took the ball.

"Obstruction!" the referee called. "Foul."

Lola's team had the ball once again. Nathaniel was delighted. He admired the way she played — good teamwork and strategy. She was also a beautiful runner.

On the next play Lola received the ball from the center, zigzagged down the field, and scored.

"Good going, Lola," the hockey coach called.

Nathaniel moved even closer and stood behind a tree. He didn't want anyone to see him watching girls' field hockey.

Lola and the forward line were in position again. Her thick dark hair was tied into a bunch on top of her head. Loose strands were sticking to the sweat on her flushed face.

Lola brushed up the hair that was curling down her neck. Then she turned and saw Nathaniel.

Nathaniel wanted to disappear right into the earth. He ducked behind the tree, but he felt so foolish he changed his mind and walked out in front. Then he tried to rest his back casually against the tree, with his arms folded and one foot up against the trunk, but somehow he miscalculated and lost his balance. He caught himself just in time.

Lola was looking at him. Suddenly she smiled and waved. Nathaniel looked around. She was waving at him! Before he could wave back, the referee put the ball into play, and Lola turned around quickly.

The boys' gym class was supposed to be at track and field, but Nathaniel could not take his eyes off the field hockey. He could not take his eyes off Lola.

"Nathaniel!" Doug had come up behind him. "I've been looking all over for you."

Doug was wearing gym shorts, too.

Nathaniel had to think fast. "You know, Doug, girls' field hockey can be quite interesting. I was thinking about using it in a story. Well, actually . . . I was thinking of using it in a screenplay I'm working on."

"Really?" Doug, as usual, took what Nathaniel said seriously. "A screenplay?"

"Yes," Nathaniel went on. "A murder-mystery. The field hockey wouldn't be important. Just background, of course."

Doug was very interested. Together they walked to track and field discussing camera angles.

Nothing had changed between them.

Doug and Nathaniel had lunch together in the cafeteria.

"Maybe we can be lab partners even though we're in different sections of biology," Doug said.

"Let's ask," Nathaniel said. "Then we can work on some of those cures for diseases in our spare time."

Doug told Nathaniel he was planning to try out

for the swimming team after school. "But I'll call you tonight," he said.

Lola was in Nathaniel's English class, too!

He stared at the back of her head, hoping she would turn around and notice him again. He thought she was beautiful, but he wasn't sure he trusted his own judgment. "Maybe I should get a second opinion from Doug," he thought. Her fingers were long and graceful. The butterfly ring twinkled on her finger as she wrote in her notebook.

Nathaniel did not see Lola again until the end of the day. After school he went to sign up for the debate team. Nathaniel had been in the debate team in junior high school.

Sign-up sheets for extracurricular activities were posted on the bulletin board outside the library. Lola was waiting on line, holding her cello case.

Nathaniel figured that this might be a good time to tell her his father played the cello, too.

He went and stood behind her. She didn't see him. He thought he might tap her on the shoulder, but he didn't think tapping someone on the shoulder was a very "cool" way of getting that person's attention.

But, since his voice did not seem to be working, he stood by while Lola went to the board and signed her name on a list. Nathaniel was next on line.

As soon as Lola had finished, he took out his ballpoint pen, walked up to the board, and signed his name, too, under hers.

There was no place for a telephone number so he wrote his telephone number next to his name.

At the top of the next column were the words NAME OF INSTRUMENT.

Nathaniel suddenly realized he was signing up for tryouts for the high school orchestra. The people behind him in line were watching him impatiently. Nathaniel wrote "Cello" under NAME OF INSTRUMENT.

Nathaniel did not play the cello, but he was sure he could learn. His father ought to be able to give him some lessons before Friday. He would be good enough to fake his way through the tryouts, he thought. Then he and Lola would sit in the same section. It would be an easy way to get to know her.

Lola's telephone number was next to her name. Nathaniel memorized it. As soon as he got outside, he sat down on the school steps and wrote it on the back of his hand. 236 – 4758.

He tucked his hand into his windbreaker pocket and started on his way home.

Chapter VIII

A Present from Nathaniel

At the end of the day Angela waited with her friend Mandy on the bench in the playground. Angela was waiting for Nathaniel, and Mandy was waiting for her sister, who was the same age as Nathaniel.

Angela had never met Mandy's older sister, but she wanted to. She had been to Mandy's house twice and she had peeked into the sister's room. She had been very impressed with the hammock, the dressing table with three mirrors, and the large collection of cactus plants.

"Guess what," Mandy said. "We got a new puppy. My sister went home to get it. She's bringing it here. We're going to take it for its first walk. Maybe you can come with us."

"Not today," Angela said. She kept her eyes away from the lot in back of the school. The power drills and the bulldozer were silent now. Angela tried not to think about the hole in the ground where Eddie's house used to be.

Cheryl White was waiting to be picked up, too. She came and sat down next to Angela.

"Maybe they're not in the poorhouse," she said thoughtfully. "Maybe Eddie's grandmother inherited a whole bunch of money and they're living in a fancy house right now."

Angela nodded. She had thought of that possibility.

"There's Phoebe!" Mandy suddenly said and she stood up.

Angela looked at the girl coming in the school gate.

Phoebe had dark hair like Mandy's, and very rosy cheeks. She was carrying their new puppy.

"What kind of dog is that?" Cheryl wanted to know.

"It's a Cardigan Welsh corgi," Mandy's sister said and she put the puppy down on the ground.

It was a red puppy with pointy ears and short legs. She looked very alert, and interested in everything going on around her.

"How come her feet turn out?" Cheryl wanted to know.

Phoebe laughed. "That's the way these dogs are built. Even though she has short legs and turned-out feet, she'll grow up to be a very fast runner."

Cheryl reached down and petted the puppy. She pulled her hand away.

"I like silky dogs better," she said.

"These corgis have double coats," Phoebe said. "The outer hairs are supposed to be a little coarse. She's a waterproof dog."

Angela did not want to frighten the puppy, so she sat still and held out her hand. The puppy came over and sniffed it.

"I see you know something about dogs," Phoebe said to Angela. Angela felt very pleased. She thought Mandy's sister was lovely. She wished Nathaniel would hurry up so he could meet her. Then all four of them could take the puppy for a walk.

Phoebe sat down next to Angela. She didn't

seem to be in any hurry. "Is someone picking you up?" she asked.

Angela nodded. "My brother is."

"Would you like us to wait with you?" Phoebe asked.

Angela felt shy. She shook her head. "You don't have to," she said. "He'll be here soon."

Angela waited and waited, but Nathaniel did not come. At four-thirty Angela was alone on the bench. She did not know whether to worry about Eddie or Nathaniel. Miss Mason came over a few times to ask Angela if she was all right.

Angela nodded, but she did not feel all right. Her heart was beating fast. What had happened to her brother?

The sky had turned dark. Big raindrops were falling. Angela put on her raincoat.

"Maybe I should take you into the principal's office so you can call home," Miss Mason suggested.

Angela did not want to go into the principal's office. She wanted Nathaniel to come.

It was beginning to rain hard.

Just then she saw Nathaniel coming in the gate.

He was soaking wet, but he was not wearing his windbreaker. He had it draped over his hand.

"Hi, I'm sorry I'm late. I was almost home before I remembered," he said.

Angela was very happy to see her brother.

Nathaniel seemed in very good spirits.

Angela stared at the windbreaker over his hand. "Did you hurt your hand?" she asked.

"I can't get my hand wet. Quick. We've got to get to the stationery store right away."

"Why?" Angela asked.

"I need an address book," Nathaniel told her.

They ran two blocks to the stationery store. Angela looked around the store while Nathaniel bought himself a black address book. He paid for it and then carefully copied the number from his hand into the address book.

He seemed very pleased with himself.

"Would you like anything?" he asked Angela.

Angela had been admiring a small white plastic diary. MY DIARY, it said on the cover. It had blue and red balloons on it and a small lock and key.

Nathaniel looked at her. "Would you like that?"

"It costs six dollars and ninety-five cents," Angela said. Even though Angela had a steady job entertaining a cat, most of her money went to the support of an orphan in another country named Flor Elena. Angela's family donated seventeen dollars each month to the Rescue the Children Committee.

To her surprise, Nathaniel bought it for her.

It was now raining so hard, they had to wait under the awning in front of the store. Nathaniel seemed to be in another world.

"Angela," he said in a dreamy voice. "Do you think two people can be destined for each other?"

Angela stared at the rain beating down on the sidewalk. She had a funny feeling in her stomach.

"Do you think somewhere in this world there is only one person who is meant for you?" Nathaniel asked.

Angela got the shivers.

"Think of it," Nathaniel said. "Just one in five billion."

Angela nodded. She had goose bumps on her arms.

Chapter IX

An Evening at Home

Angela sat in the living room that evening and waited for the phone to ring. She was hoping Miss Mason would call and tell her that Eddie was living close by in a nice new house — and that he would be back in class tomorrow.

But every time the telephone rang, it was somebody else. Mrs. Glenn called and told Tina's mother she was going to stop by with some brochures about the ballroom dancing lessons at the Tudor Classes.

Tina's mother thought it sounded like a wonderful idea. "I went to ballroom dancing lessons when I was your age, Tina. It's not so expensive."

"You mean I can go?" Tina asked.

"Don't you want to?" her mother asked.

Tina was curled up on the couch reading. "I don't know," Tina murmured. "I don't think so. It sounds too scary."

"Well, you could wait and start in January," her mother said. "Would you like to do that?"

Tina grunted. She was concentrating on her book. Her mother studied her for a moment. Then she noticed the jacket of the book. It was a hardcover.

"Oh, you're reading *Silas Marner!*" she said. "That's a wonderful book. I loved it. Is it an English assignment?"

Tina nodded, but she never looked up.

Nathaniel and his father were engaged in a long discussion as to whether or not Nathaniel could learn to play the cello in four days.

"Believe me, Nathaniel. I'd do anything I could to teach you," his father said, "but I'm afraid it simply can't be done. Why are you suddenly so interested in learning the cello? What about the debate team? Didn't you sign up for that?"

Nathaniel shook his head. He seemed very discouraged.

The phone rang again. This time it was Doug.

Angela could hear Nathaniel saying, over and over, "Oh, that's great. That's great," but he didn't sound very happy.

"What's going on?" Tina took her nose out of her book. "Are you and Doug friends again? Is he coming over?"

"Of course we're friends. We're going to be lab partners, too," Nathaniel said. He sighed. "Doug made the swimming team. He's going to be busy every afternoon."

"That's great!" Tina said, but she didn't sound happy either.

Nathaniel went to do his homework, and their father went to practice his cello.

Mrs. Glenn rang the intercom at eight o'clock.

"She's coming up here?" Tina wailed. "I thought she was going to drop those brochures off with the doorman."

"What's wrong with her coming up here?" her mother asked. "She's never been here."

"That's what I mean!" Tina looked around the living room. "What is she going to *think*?" Then she said abruptly, "Don't let her in."

"Don't be silly, Tina," her mother said.

Angela had been to Melissa's house once. Everything was perfect. There were paintings on the wall, lots of white furniture and glass tables. . . .

"Our living room is nice, too," Angela thought. "It's just different."

"I'm getting out of here," Tina said. "Tell her I'm asleep."

"Tina!" her mother said. But Tina had left the room. Angela's mother went to open the door.

Mrs. Glenn walked in and put her finger delicately to her ear. "Ah, the strains of a cello. You are so fortunate to be married to a musician."

She smiled at Angela and ruffled her hair. "Aren't we getting big?"

Mrs. Glenn looked very glamorous in a black satin suit with gold embroidery on the jacket. She handed Angela's mother a folder. "We're meeting some people for dinner and I wanted to drop this off on the way."

"Would you like to come in?"

"I only have a minute." Mrs. Glenn went into the living room and looked around.

"Well, isn't this *comfortable*," she said.

Then she said it again. "Well, isn't this *comfortable*."

Angela's mother thanked Mrs. Glenn for bringing the information on the Tudor Classes. Then she explained that Tina wasn't ready to go to dancing classes. "She wants to wait until January."

Mrs. Glenn seemed disappointed, but she said, "Well, I suppose Tina has always been a slow-developer compared to Melissa."

"I don't know about that," Angela heard her mother say a bit sharply.

"Well, as it turns out, three of Melissa's friends from camp are joining the ballroom dancing classes this fall, so Melissa feels more comfortable about going." Mrs. Glenn suddenly turned. "There are scholarships available, in case . . ."

"That's not necessary," Angela's mother said coldly.

Just then Mrs. Glenn noticed the book on the table. It was lying facedown, opened to the page

Tina was reading when she so hastily fled.

"*Silas Marner?*" Mrs. Glenn breathed. "How gorgeous. I simply adored that book."

"Tina's reading it," Angela heard her mother say a little proudly. "It's an English assignment."

"I don't understand. Melissa hasn't mentioned it. And I believe they have the same English teacher."

Mrs. Glenn was looking at the book so lovingly, Angela was afraid she was going to drool on it. "Ah, George Eliot. What a magnificent writer. What a beautiful prose style. She certainly knew how to use the English language."

"*She?*" Angela thought.

Mrs. Glenn picked the book up and read the page Tina was reading.

She sighed. "I remember this part so well. I almost know it by heart. Just listen to the music of these words," and she read out loud in a lilting voice with a bit of an English accent.

" 'The smell of magnolias in her jet-black hair wafted across the heavy night air. The moon was rising and casting a spell over his senses. . . .' "

Mrs. Glenn stopped. "Oh, do forgive me," she said. "I guess I got a little carried away. But I'm so pleased that our young people are being introduced to great literature."

Mrs. Glenn said good-night and sailed out the door. Angela's mother went into the living room and stood there looking at the book.

"Where in the world did Tina get this?" Very carefully she took off the dust jacket that said *Silas Marner*. She studied the spine.

"*Island Romance*," she read. She looked on the inside. "This is the property of Cecily H. Simon."

She looked at Angela. "Isn't that Melissa's housekeeper?" Then very carefully, she put the dust jacket back on.

"Are you going to say anything to Tina?" Angela whispered.

Her mother shrugged. "I don't know. I remember doing something like this myself when I was Tina's age," she said. Then to Angela's surprise, she sank down on the couch and began to laugh. "*Silas Marner* . . . was about a penny-pinching old . . . miser," she told Angela.

"But Melissa's mother said she remembered the part about that lady's hair smelling like magnolias."

"I don't think she ever read *Silas Marner*. I think she was faking!" Angela's mother hugged a pillow and howled with laughter.

Angela began to laugh. "And she called George Eliot 'she.'" Angela was pleased that she, too, could see through Mrs. Glenn.

"What's so funny?" Her father was standing in the doorway.

"We can't tell," Angela giggled.

"You two are being silly," he said.

Her father looked so left out, Angela said, "Melissa's mother called George Eliot 'she.'"

"Well, she was," her father said. "George Eliot was a woman. You knew that, dear." He gave his wife a puzzled look.

That only made Angela and her mother laugh harder.

Angela felt better. She went to her room and put her BISY sign up on the door. She took out her new diary and opened it.

Dear Diary, (she wrote)
    Eddie is not at school yet.
His house isn't there. Nobody
knows where is his new
house. Not even the teachers.
I guess he will be back
tomorrow. There is a new
boy. His name is Luther.
I do not like Luther.

Then Angela got a better idea. She turned the
page and wrote:

My Wedding Diary
Bride = Angela Steele
Broom = Eddie Bishop.

She thought a minute and wrote:

Buget for the Wedding

Her parents were always talking about keeping track of money. Angela wanted to be practical, too.

Angela was pleased. She would work on her wedding plans until Eddie came back.

Angela read over what she had written. It was enough work for one night. Angela closed her diary and went to brush her teeth.

Nathaniel was lying on his bed, staring up at the ceiling. Angela said good-night, but he didn't seem to hear her. She tiptoed away.

Suddenly she heard him say, "A xylophone! I should have put that down. I bet I could learn to play a xylophone in a couple of hours!"

Chapter X

Worries

Angela was worried about her brother. Nathaniel had become very quiet.

Every day he picked up Angela right after school. They walked straight home, and Nathaniel went right to his room. Sometimes he did his homework, and sometimes he just lay on his bed, staring up at the ceiling and listening to music.

Angela knew her parents were worried about him, too.

He had crossed off his name for the school orchestra tryouts, but he had not signed up for anything else.

"Maybe it would be a good idea to get involved

in something after school," his mother suggested every once in a while.

"Too much homework," was all Nathaniel would say.

Nathaniel came to pick Angela up each day before Mandy's sister arrived. Angela was disappointed. She wanted them to meet each other. They were both in the same grade in high school, but Nathaniel said he didn't know anyone named Phoebe.

On Halloween Mandy and her sister showed up for the Block Fair on Angela's street. Angela wanted to introduce her brother to Mandy's sister. But Nathaniel had a complicated costume, which took all his attention. He kept changing from Dr. Jekyll, the quiet scientist, to Mr. Hyde, the insane murderer — and back again. He even managed to grow long nails by hiding his father's plastic collar stays under the sleeves of his shirt. Nathaniel had perfected this costume over the years.

To make matters worse, Mandy's sister was dressed in a gorilla outfit. Angela didn't think it would be much use for Nathaniel to meet a girl dressed in a gorilla outfit.

Mandy invited Angela to her house a few times, but Angela said "no." She didn't want Nathaniel to be lonely.

Nathaniel seemed to need Angela's company. He even told Angela she could do her homework at his desk.

Angela felt very cozy in his room. She enjoyed listening to his records — especially the old cowboy songs he played over and over again.

But Nathaniel never talked about what was bothering him.

The rest of the house was quiet. Tina always had her nose buried in a book. "Another great classic," Angela heard her mother say with a giggle.

Angela was not enjoying school. Every afternoon she counted the minutes until school would be over.

For the first time in her life, she was afraid of her teacher. For a large woman, Miss Blizzard moved quickly. She always seemed to be looming up when Angela least expected her.

Miss Blizzard also called on people. Angela was always terrified that she would not be ready with the right answer when the teacher called her name. And, to her distress, Miss Blizzard never seemed to call on her when she *did* know the answer; only when she didn't.

For this reason Angela had decided that Miss Blizzard could read children's minds. She would often catch Miss Blizzard looking at her, and she would try to clear her mind of all thoughts Miss Blizzard would not approve of. She would try to make her mind a complete blank.

Silent reading time had become a nightmare. Angela could not make any sense out of the book she had chosen. Now, she found there were more books mixed in with *The Wizard of Oz*. There was another book called *The Council of the Munchkins*. The title of that book now appeared on the top of every right-hand page. Angela tried to ignore that book, too.

Book reports were beginning to appear on the bulletin board as other children in her class finished the books they were reading. "But they're all baby books," Angela told herself.

"Let me know if any of you need help," Miss Blizzard said one day. "Remember, that is what I am here for." She was looking right at Angela.

Angela had no intention of asking anyone for

help. She would figure it out for herself.

She looked down at the book again and forced her eyes quickly along the lines. She moved her eyebrows up and down, trying to look surprised and interested at the same time.

"Why are you making those funny faces?" Luther whispered. "You look weird."

Luther was becoming a pest. He seemed to enjoy picking on Angela. He knocked her pencils off her desk; he repeated everything she said under his breath. He always seemed to be making fun of her.

Chris seemed to find Luther's imitations of Angela very funny. Together they followed her around, calling her Angela Old Bean and playing mean tricks on her.

Angela could not even take a drink of water at the water fountain without either Luther or Chris squirting water all over her.

Angela tried to ignore both of them, but the more she ignored them the more Luther tormented her.

The day before Thanksgiving, Miss Blizzard told Angela she could take *The Wizard of Oz* home over the holiday. Angela decided she would try reading it to Moxie.

Moxie curled up on the arm of the chair and waited for Angela to begin. Angela showed Moxie the map of the Land of Oz and the picture of Dorothy, the tin woodsman, and the scarecrow.

"But that's another book," Angela explained, pointing to the book called *The Cyclone* on the right-hand page.

Before Angela could turn the page, Moxie suddenly stretched out both paws and held the page down. She stared right into Angela's eyes. Then she slowly pulled herself up and sat down right in the middle of the page that said *The Cyclone*.

Angela pulled the book out from under Moxie and moved it to the other arm of the chair. She studied the page Moxie had been sitting on. It was all about Dorothy and Auntie Em.

Angela turned back and looked at the List of Chapters. "Moxie!" she breathed. "You solved the mystery. It's all one book! *The Cyclone* is the name of the first chapter! It's all *The Wizard of Oz*!"

Angela was delighted. When she got back to school she started the book all over from the beginning.

The week before Christmas she learned from Cheryl that Luther was working on a "fiendish invention." Angela was to be the target.

All week she had seen Luther drawing plans and showing them to Chris. All she could see was that the invention had something to do with shoes.

Luther was so proud of his invention that word got around. On the day before Christmas vacation, Angela found out that Luther was designing shoes with mirrors attached so that he could see up her dress! All the boys in the class were impressed with the brilliance of this idea. To Angela's horror, they were making bets on the color of her underpants.

Unfortunately, on that particular day, Angela was wearing an old pair of Nathaniel's jockey shorts. Her mother was behind in the laundry.

Angela could think of nothing else all day. When silent reading time came, she held the book in front of her and kept her eyes on the clock.

She didn't even see Miss Blizzard until her large figure loomed above her.

"Isn't it about time you talked about the problem you are having?" Miss Blizzard said.

By now Angela was so sure Miss Blizzard could read children's minds, she assumed Miss Blizzard was talking about Nathaniel's jockey shorts.

But Miss Blizzard was staring at the book.

Angela suddenly realized she had been holding *The Wizard of Oz* upside down.

In front of the whole class Miss Blizzard took *The Wizard of Oz* away from Angela and told her to go up and see the librarian about finding her something more "appropriate for her reading level."

Angela did what she was told and returned to class with *Make Way for Ducklings*.

But she was having trouble reading it. Every page was a blur. Her eyes kept filling up with tears.

Luther kept turning around to look at her. Angela wanted to tell him to mind his own business until she noticed that he had tears in his eyes, too.

All during Christmas vacation Angela worked out her wedding plans. She designed the wedding cake; she made a list of her guests. She tried to decide who should marry them. Her mother had once told her that the captain of a ship could marry people. Angela thought that it would be nice to have her wedding on the ferry that went around the harbor.

For some reason Angela had come to believe that Eddie Bishop would be back right after Christmas. The first day of school she looked all over for him, but he wasn't there. A parking garage was being built in the lot behind the school.

Chapter XI

The Telephone Call

On the second Friday in January, Tina was going to begin ballroom dancing classes.

"Melissa is actually enjoying them, even though she says she's not interested in anyone in the class," she told the family. "The boys are very immature, Melissa says. Besides, Rocky would be furious with her if she got interested in anyone else."

The first night Tina was very nervous. "No one's going to ask me to dance," she kept saying, and, "I feel ridiculous."

Tina was all dressed up in a blue satin dress with a dark green velvet sash. Her hair was pulled back with a small green bow. She was wearing white gloves. Angela thought her sister looked beautiful.

It wasn't a new dress. When Aunt Patty had heard about Tina's ballroom dancing lessons, she sent a trunk of her clothes that she had kept since sixth grade. The blue satin dress was Tina's favorite.

"Your hair smells like flowers," Angela said.

"Magnolias," Tina told her. "Melissa let me use some of her magnolia perfume."

The lessons started at six. Melissa's mother was supposed to pick Tina up at five-thirty. "She always stays and watches!" Tina said. "Can you imagine how Melissa feels about that?"

"I'd love to watch sometime," her mother said with a smile.

"No!" Tina said. "Never. Mom, promise me you'll never watch."

"Well . . ."

The doorbell rang. It was Doug. Doug usually came over on Friday nights. He and Nathaniel would spend hours discussing which movie they wanted to see — usually science fiction or adventure. Sometimes they spent so long making up their minds, they missed the starting time.

"Wow, Tina," he said. "You look fantastic."

Tina groaned. "But I feel ridiculous," she said.

After Doug had left the living room, Angela heard her mother tell Tina, "When you get a compliment like that, it's a good idea to just smile and say, 'Thank you.' "

Tina groaned. "I just wish tonight were over."

The buzzer rang from downstairs; Tina jumped up. "I'm going to have a horrible time," she said as she went out the door. "I know it."

A few minutes later, Doug left.

"Where's he going?" their mother asked.

"To a party," Nathaniel said. "I was invited, too, I guess, but I just don't feel like going."

"Oh, Nathaniel," their mother said sadly.

Angela's father had a concert that night.

"Will you keep an eye on Angela?" their mother asked Nathaniel. "I told your father I'd go to the concert."

"Sure," Nathaniel said.

Angela waited until she heard the door to Nathaniel's room close. She tiptoed into her parents' bedroom. She did not turn on the light. There were three long windows in the corner of the room. The windows were covered with long white gauzy curtains that almost touched the floor. Tonight there was a full moon.

Angela wrapped herself in the white curtains. By the light of the moon, she could see her reflection in the long mirror on the door of her parents' closet. Angela was pretending she was a bride.

She danced and swirled in the long curtains.

Suddenly the bedroom light went on. Angela stopped and stood still. . . . Nathaniel had come into the room. She was tangled up in the curtains. She held her breath and listened.

Her parents' telephone was on the night table. Angela could hear her brother dialing.

"Hello?" she heard him ask. "Is Lola home? (Pause) May I speak to her? It's Nathaniel. Nathaniel Steele. Yes, thank you. I'll wait."

A moment later he said, "That's okay, I can hold on."

It seemed like a very long time.

"Hello, Lola? This is Nathaniel. Um . . . Nathaniel Steele . . . Nathaniel. I'm in your homeroom. Your biology class, too."

There was another pause.

"No, I don't wear glasses. That's Mark. I sit right behind Mark." (Pause)

"Oh . . . you don't remember. . . . Well, I'm in your English class, too. I have sort of brown hair."

Angela crossed her fingers and hoped that this girl Lola would remember her brother.

"Not too tall, well, a little tall. I wear this T-shirt, sometimes. . . . I'm the one who used to watch you play hockey."

Angela could not believe that any girl would not notice her brother.

"Oh, I see . . . you don't remember."

Angela felt crushed.

"Well, anyway," Nathaniel went on. "I was wondering if you would like to go to the movies with me next Friday night . . . um, you see . . ."

Nathaniel was quiet. He was listening.

"Oh, I see. You're busy. Well, how about the Friday after that . . ."

A pause.

"Busy again? And the Friday after that?"

"I see . . . I see . . ." Nathaniel kept saying.

Angela held her breath and tried to figure out

what this Lola was saying. Nathaniel was listening for what seemed to Angela a very long time.

Finally he cleared his throat and said, "I see . . . oh yes, you've made it perfectly clear, but . . . um . . . let's put it this way: What if hell does freeze over?"

Angela gasped.

Another pause.

"Not even then? I see . . . I see . . ."

A moment later she heard Nathaniel hang up.

Angela was so ashamed of the way this girl had treated her brother, she hated her. How could anyone be so cruel?

Angela wanted revenge. "I'll track her down," Angela told herself. "I'll give her tiny pinches, the ones that really hurt. I'll crack raw eggs into her hair. I'll jump up and down on her. . . ."

Angela's heart was filled with violence.

She made a sudden movement. The curtain rods slipped off their hooks, and the curtains fell down on top of her.

The next minute Nathaniel was untangling her from the curtains.

"What are you doing here, Angela?" he asked.

"What's the matter? Why is your face so red?"

"I heard," Angela murmured.

"What did you hear?" Nathaniel asked. He seemed almost amused.

"What that girl said," Angela whispered. "That girl, Lola. The one who won't go out with you."

Nathaniel looked at Angela and grinned. Angela couldn't understand it.

"Angela, it wasn't a real telephone call. I had my finger on the button the whole time. It was a practice call. I was just pretending to call her."

"Oh," Angela said. "You mean Lola wasn't really on the phone?" She was still having trouble sorting it out. "You were only pretending?"

"Yes," Nathaniel said. "I do it all the time. I guess it's become kind of an 'act.' " Then he said, "Listen, Angela, don't tell anyone."

"I won't," Angela promised.

Nathaniel said, "What were you doing in here?"

"Playing . . . playing . . . ghost," Angela said. "Practicing for next Halloween." She thought it sounded better than the truth.

Later that evening, Angela and Nathaniel were drying the dishes.

"Nathaniel," Angela said in a very small voice. "Is Lola really nice?"

Nathaniel sighed. "Really nice. Beautiful, too. You see, I think she liked me the first day of school, but I kind of missed my chance." He sighed again. "I guess our relationship has gone downhill ever since — if you can call it 'a relationship.' We've never even talked to each other. I'm not sure if she even notices me anymore."

Angela wanted to help.

"Maybe you could send her a Valentine," Angela suggested. "Valentine's Day is only twenty-nine days away."

Angela was counting the days until the weekend that she would be completely in charge of Moxie.

"I don't think I can send her a Valentine," Nathaniel said. "If I don't sign my name, she'll never guess who it is, and if I do, she'll think I'm in love with her or something."

Nathaniel looked so miserable, Angela changed the subject. "Does she . . . um . . . ever say 'yes' when you make a practice telephone call?" Angela wanted to know.

Nathaniel's face turned red. "Yes, sometimes, but it's just as bad. Then I wonder what I would talk about on a date."

"If you took her to a movie, you wouldn't have to talk very much," Angela said.

Nathaniel sighed. "She'd probably say 'no.' "

"Maybe she would say 'yes,' " Angela said after a while.

"Do you think I should call her?" Nathaniel asked.

"Yes," Angela said.

Nathaniel shook his head. "I'm not ready. You see, right now I'm a nobody in that school. I have to do something important first. I have to make an impression so everyone notices me and knows who I am. I have to make a splash."

"A splash?" Angela asked nervously. She hoped Nathaniel wasn't planning on making up any more Bible stories.

"A big splash," Nathaniel said. "Then I can ask her out."

Chapter XII

A Scandal

Angela had her doubts about Lola. She had never met Lola. She wasn't sure Lola was worthy of her brother. And she was sure, if Nathaniel met Mandy's sister, he would never look at Lola again.

Monday was a snowy day. After school Angela left her boots in the closet of her classroom on purpose. She went to sit on the bench in the playground with Mandy.

"How's Phoebe?" Angela asked.

"Good," Mandy said.

"Is she coming here after school?"

"Yes," Mandy said.

When Nathaniel arrived, Angela told him she

had forgotten her boots. She asked him to wait for her in the playground.

Angela went back into the school. She skipped up and down the halls for a while to give Nathaniel and Phoebe a chance to meet.

". . . By now they will have fallen in love," she told herself. She went to find a window in the hallway that overlooked the playground. She saw Mandy, Phoebe, and the puppy walking out the gate, but she didn't see Nathaniel at all.

A few minutes later she heard Nathaniel's voice. She found him in the kindergarten classroom talking Miss Berry's ear off, telling her his impressions of high school.

That night she found Nathaniel sitting at his desk reading the love letters from the girls at camp. He was copying their names and phone numbers into his black address book.

"Are you going to call Nora?" Angela asked when she noticed the envelope that said SEALED WITH A KISS.

Nathaniel shook his head. "I just want to fill up my address book with girls' names," he said. "It looks empty. The only phone number I have is Lola's."

Nathaniel seemed very depressed. "I think Lola likes this guy David. He's her lab partner and goes around in this denim jacket and thinks he's cool. I saw her talking to him in the hall."

Later that evening Angela even heard him ask Tina for Melissa's phone number.

"What for?" Tina asked suspiciously.

"I'm just bringing my address book up-to-date," Nathaniel said.

"Maybe Nathaniel should take ballroom dancing lessons," Tina said one night at dinner. "It might help him get over his shyness with girls, and it's really fun."

"I'm not the least bit shy and I don't want to learn how to dance," Nathaniel said.

"We learn these really neat steps," Tina went on, "and the boys in the class aren't so bad. Of course the ones who ask me to dance are all shorter than I am."

The only thing Tina didn't like was the car ride home from classes every Friday night.

"Mrs. Glenn tells Melissa everything she did wrong, and Melissa sulks. Then all her snobby friends from camp — Lila and Stephanie and

Chickie — talk about how many times they were cut in on. You, see, there are extra boys and they are allowed to cut in on your partner in the middle of a dance. They keep score. And they always ask Mrs. Glenn to drop me off first."

"Why do they do that?" her mother asked.

"So they can talk about me behind my back, I guess." Tina shrugged.

After each dance class Tina gave Angela dance lessons. She showed Angela the waltz, the cha-cha, and the lindy. Angela liked the lindy best of all. Angela in turn gave Moxie a few dance lessons.

Lately Angela only felt happy when she was with Moxie. She loved Moxie, and Moxie loved her. Angela was looking forward to taking care of Moxie all by herself on Valentine's Day weekend. Madeline was giving her lessons in opening cat food cans, changing kitty litter, and turning the key in the front door to open it and lock it. . . .

"I'm teaching you new skills," Madeline said, "so don't expect me to pay you extra for doing my job when I'm away."

"That's okay," Angela said. "Twenty-five cents for the weekend is all I want."

"With these additional skills," Madeline went on, "you will always be able to get a job."

"I know that," Angela said.

Angela met Moxie's owners, Tony and Pamela. "It's fine with us," Tony said. "Angela seems like a very responsible little girl."

When Angela heard that, she told her mother she did not want a birthday party this year.

"I have too much to do that weekend," she said. "I have a full-time job."

The first week in February there was a scandal.

It was a "deep dark secret," but Tina kept Angela up-to-date on every detail.

One of Melissa's camp friends had called Rocky and told him that Melissa was going around with a bracelet with his name on it. She asked Rocky if he and Melissa were really going steady.

Rocky's mother then called Mrs. Glenn and told her to "Put a stop to this nonsense." Her son was far too young to go steady. As a matter of fact, he didn't even remember dancing with anyone named Melissa.

Tina said she felt very sorry for Melissa, who

stayed home from school and cried for a whole day.

Tina brought Melissa her homework assignment. "She looks terrible," she told Angela. "There are big circles under her eyes, and her hair is a complete mess." Tina almost sounded gleeful. "Believe it or not, she's still in love with Rocky, and she said she might be losing her mind."

"Why?" Angela asked.

"Because love can drive you crazy," Tina said. She then told Angela the entire plot of *By Passion Possessed*, another novel that belonged to Melissa's housekeeper.

"Melissa read it, too," Tina said. "Melissa said she would never show her face in public again. She said she was 'through with men.' "

Angela was very impressed.

But the next Friday night, Melissa fell madly in love with Jake, an older boy in the ballroom class. "He cut in on me twice," she boasted in the car. . . .

. . . And that Saturday night, Melissa came over and spent the whole evening talking to Nathaniel and Doug — but mostly to Doug.

The next morning Angela awoke and found Tina sitting on the side of her bed. "Did you hear Melissa laughing at every single thing Doug said?" Tina was close to tears. "By the end of the night, Doug was only talking to Melissa. He forgot I was even there. It's not fair. I hate her."

Angela did not blame Tina a bit.

Angela did not write a word in her Wedding Diary all weekend. And she only sent one Valentine — to her orphan, Flor Elena. "Guess Who?" she wrote. Then in parenthesis she wrote "(Angela)" just in case Flor Elena did not know about Valentines. She spent the rest of the time working on her plans for the School for Cats.

Angela was beginning to think love was a pretty gloomy business — dangerous, too!

Chapter XIII

Warning Signs

Nathaniel was in a strange mood that Sunday. Angela saw him sitting on the floor of his room going through all the ads in the Sunday paper. He seemed desperate about something. "I've got to find it," he kept saying. "It's got to be perfect." He kept running his hands through his hair.

He looked up and saw Angela. Angela thought he had a wild look in his eyes. He looked like he was in the middle of his transformation from Dr. Jekyll to Mr. Hyde. She wondered if he was "losing his mind."

"Angela, help me," he said. "Go out in the hall

and see if there are any other newspapers. Look on every floor of the building."

Angela went into the kitchen and asked her mother if it would be all right to do that.

"I guess so," her mother said. "What does Nathaniel need them for?"

Angela shrugged. "An assignment."

"Take the laundry cart," her mother suggested.

A half an hour later, Angela wheeled in a shopping cart full of old newspapers.

Nathaniel put them on the living room table. He started going through them.

"This is my big chance," he muttered to himself. "This is my chance to make a big splash."

He noticed Angela staring up at him. "What's the matter?" he asked. "Why are you staring at me?"

"What are you doing?" Angela whispered.

Nathaniel took a deep breath and spoke in the calm reasonable tones of Dr. Jekyll. "It's simple. We have this English assignment. Nothing unusual about it. We're supposed to cut out an advertisement and pretend to send away for something. We're learning about writing business letters. All I have to do is find an ad, but it's got to be the right ad. It's got to be perfect."

"What ad are you looking for?" Angela asked.

To Angela's surprise, Nathaniel suddenly pounded his fist on the table. "I don't know!" he shouted. "I wish I knew!"

Angela tried to be calm. She suspected that Nathaniel's love for Lola was driving him mad.

The next minute Nathaniel was speaking once again in the quiet voice of Dr. Jekyll.

"Don't you see?" he said. "I know what the teacher is going to tell us to do next."

Right before Angela's eyes, Nathaniel was changing again into Mr. Hyde. He began rubbing his hands together. His eyes gleamed, and he began to laugh. To Angela's ears his laugh sounded more like a cackle.

"Don't you see?" Nathaniel said in a harsh horrible whisper. "I have guessed the next assignment. I woke up this morning and all of a sudden it came to me! Written on a blackboard right before my eyes! A vision!"

"What will the next assignment be?" Angela asked politely.

"Are you ready for this?" Nathaniel asked.

Angela nodded.

Nathaniel closed his eyes and recited, " 'Write a formal letter of complaint about the item you ordered from the advertisement in the newspaper.' " He opened his eyes and stared at Angela.

"That's nice," Angela said, and she decided that Lola was definitely bad for her brother.

That evening Angela's mother asked her if she had changed her mind about having a birthday party. "What if you just invited one or two friends for a little party Friday evening. We could have an early supper. You would have plenty of time for Moxie."

Angela suddenly had an idea. "Maybe I *would* like a party," she said slowly. "But I just want Mandy and one other person," she said, ". . . and only if Nathaniel comes to the party and does his Great Waldo the Magician act."

Her mother looked over at Nathaniel, who was still tearing through the newspapers. "I'm sure Nathaniel would be delighted."

"Huh?" Nathaniel asked.

Angela explained, and Nathaniel said, "Oh, yeah, sure. Sounds great," and went back to the newspapers.

That night Angela wrote two invitations. "You are corjully invited to a birthday party and Magic Show. . . ." she began. One she addressed to Mandy, and the other to Mandy's sister Phoebe.

As she was sealing the envelopes, she heard Nathaniel shout, "I found it! I got it!"

Angela hoped her brother wasn't going to get much worse before Friday.

She brought the invitations to school the next day. After school she handed them to Mandy.

"It's my birthday," she whispered. "I'm only inviting you two."

Mandy looked at the envelopes. "Are you sure it's all right with your mother for Phoebe to come, too?" she asked.

"Of course," Angela said.

Mandy was very pleased. Angela felt very clever for having finally thought of a way for Nathaniel to meet Mandy's sister.

"By the way, how is Phoebe?" Angela asked.

Mandy sighed. "She's been bad."

"Bad?" Angela asked.

"My parents are talking about getting rid of her," Mandy said.

Angela was shocked. She knew Mandy's

mother was strict. The time Angela had been at Mandy's house for a play date, her mother had yelled at her for breaking her crayons. But it seemed a little extreme for Mandy's parents to want to get rid of their eldest daughter.

"What did she do?" Angela asked.

"Well, nobody knew it, but for months she's been chewing through the bottom of my parents' mattress. She was working on the slats, too. Last night they fell through onto the floor."

Chewing through the mattress? Angela was no longer sure Phoebe was the right girl for her brother. But then again, when she thought of the wild look in Nathaniel's eyes . . .

Suddenly she realized that she had misunderstood right from the first day of school.

"Phoebe, the dog, right?" Angela asked.

Mandy giggled. "That's the only Phoebe in my family," she said.

Chapter XIV

Not-a-Date

Angela could not take back the birthday invitations. That would be rude. And, Angela thought, it would be even more impolite to ask Mandy her sister's name at such a late date.

Nathaniel was in a very good mood that afternoon. "I was right," he told Angela. "We have to write a letter of complaint about the item we ordered. That's our assignment for Wednesday. I guessed it almost word for word."

"What did you send away for?" Angela asked.

Nathaniel grinned. "Believe it or not, I found an ad for a parachute."

On Thursday morning Angela was very

surprised when Miss Berry stopped Nathaniel and said, "Oh, Nathaniel, I heard about your parachute letters. A friend of mine is in the high school English department. You have the whole school laughing!"

"Well, I don't know about that. . . ." Nathaniel said. Angela was surprised that her brother could look so modest.

"I heard that you put the Intensive Care Ward at St. Joseph's Hospital as the return address of the letter of complaint, and said things like, 'To my regret the parachute proved to have a slight defect. . . .' He said it was very subtle humor."

Nathaniel looked very pleased. That afternoon he told Angela that Lola had laughed her head off.

"She has this amazing laugh," he said. "At first you might think she sounds like a horse, but it's not really a snort; it's more musical. After lunch she came up to me and told me my business letter was the funniest thing she had ever read. And we ended up talking on the school steps for almost twenty minutes."

"What did you talk about?" Angela asked.

"Things," Nathaniel said happily. "She loves science fiction movies, but she hasn't seen any new wave science fiction. She hasn't even seen *The Revolt of the Main Frames*."

Angela knew that Nathaniel and Doug had already seen that movie six times.

"Did you invite her to the movies?" Angela asked.

"I didn't exactly invite her to the movies," Nathaniel said, "but I told her I had to see that movie again, and I just happened to be going tomorrow night, and I was interested in her opinion of this one particular scene. . . . I mean it isn't a date or anything like that, but she's going to meet me at the seven o'clock show. I told her I'd go and get the tickets first, so it is sort of a date, even though it's not a date. . . ."

"Will you still be able to be The Great Waldo for my birthday party?" Angela was getting nervous. She still hadn't told anyone that she had invited a dog to her party.

Nathaniel said, "Oops, I forgot all about that. What time is your party?"

"Four-thirty," Angela said.

"Oh, there will be plenty of time," Nathaniel assured her. "I don't have to be at the theater until six-thirty."

That afternoon Mandy's mother called Angela's mother and told her that Phoebe had been eating a certain amount of small, but expensive jewelry lately, and she felt that Phoebe was not quite old enough to be a guest at a birthday party — especially a birthday party at someone else's house.

Angela's mother was surprised, but she said, "Well, perhaps next year."

After she hung up, she said to Angela, "Who is Phoebe?"

When Angela told her Phoebe was a puppy, her mother laughed and told her why Phoebe couldn't come.

"I thought she was only interested in mattresses," Angela said.

That evening Nathaniel kept knocking things over. He broke a plate and two glasses. At dinner he mentioned that he was meeting this girl Lola at the movies on Friday, "but it's not a date," he said.

Tina immediately called Melissa and told Melissa that Nathaniel was going on a date.

"IT'S NOT A DATE!" Nathaniel shouted.

When Tina got off the phone, their mother called Aunt Patty.

"Nathaniel is going on his first date," Angela heard her mother tell her sister.

"IT'S NOT A DATE!" Nathaniel shouted again. "DON'T CALL IT A DATE!"

After dinner Nathaniel began trying on clothes. He asked everyone in the family what they thought of each outfit.

No matter what anyone said, nothing seemed right to him.

"How late are stores open?" Nathaniel asked. "I still have the money I saved from my job at camp."

"Well, it is Thursday night," his mother said. "Some stores will be open until nine o'clock."

Nathaniel called Doug, and together they went out shopping. He came back with a large white cotton sweater, a dark blue shirt, and a new pair of blue jeans. He spent the rest of the evening in the basement washing them over and over so that they wouldn't look new.

Chapter XV

A Tight Schedule

Angela was still in her pajamas the next morning when Madeline arrived with the keys for Moxie's apartment. She handed them to Angela.

The keys were on a ring with a royal-blue medallion on it and a gold "M" for "Moxie."

"I fed Moxie breakfast," Madeline said. She studied Angela for a few seconds. "Did you turn seven yet?" she asked.

"Yes," Angela said. "I was born at five o'clock in the morning."

"I thought you looked older," Madeline said. "You've aged quite a bit lately. Your eyes look older."

When Madeline had gone, Angela carefully put the keys on the front hall table. She went back to her room, studied herself in the mirror for a while, and decided her eyes did look older. Then she sat down at her desk and went back to work on her schedule.

My Skejual

Friday, Feb. 13

Come home. Get Keys.
Open door to Moxie's.
Lock door behind.
Say hello to Moxie and
tell Moxie you will be
back at six thirty.
Lock door behind.
Come home. Put Keys
on our hall table.

Put on party dress.

Mandy comes.

Nathaniel. Great
Waldo the Magician
Act.

 Birthday dinner.
Tina leaves for dancing.
Save Tina piece of cake.

 Mandy goes home.

 Get Keys. Go to Moxies
Open door. Lock door
behind. Open can of
cat food. Change water.

Angela stopped. Nathaniel was known to be absentminded. Sometimes he was late for important occasions. What if Lola got to the theater and he wasn't there? What if they ran out of tickets?

Angela was almost as nervous about Nathaniel's date with Lola as she was about her job with Moxie.

Angela drew some more clocks and wrote a

schedule for Nathaniel, too. "NATHANIEL'S SKEJUAL," she wrote at the top. She decided he should be wearing his new outfit when Mandy arrived, just in case Mandy's sister came, too. Then he could change into his Great Waldo the Magician costume.

Angela was considering making another schedule for Tina and after that, perhaps, one big minute-by-minute schedule coordinating the movements of her entire family, when her mother called, "Time for breakfast!"

Angela put her schedule in her book bag, so she could study it when she had time.

When she got to school, she found out she had left her homework at home. She had left her milk money at home, and she had completely forgotten that today her class was bringing in Valentines. There was a mailbox sitting on the teacher's desk.

Miss Blizzard had very definite ideas about the observance of Valentine's Day.

"Remember," she said, "either you have a Valentine for everyone in the class, or none at all. I do not want anyone giving private Valentines at school."

Angela found the idea of giving Valentines to

everyone, whether you liked them or not, a bit puzzling.

Cheryl had a Valentine for everyone, and two for the teacher. She stuck them into the mailbox.

Angela was not the only one who had forgotten to bring Valentines.

"My mother said it was too expensive to give Valentines to everyone," Mandy whispered to Angela, "so I don't even have one for you."

Angela was relieved. She had no Valentine for Mandy either.

But she was surprised to see that Luther had a pile of red envelopes on his desk. They looked homemade. Luther did not seem to be the type of boy who cared about Valentine's Day.

She was even more surprised when Luther volunteered to be "the mailman" — to distribute the Valentines into each child's cubby during lunchtime.

Angela spent most of the day rehearsing her schedule for that afternoon. "Go home," she told herself. "Get keys to Moxie's. Take elevator. Open door. Lock door behind. . . ." She forgot about the Valentines until the end of the day.

She went to her cubby.

Her cubby was filled with Valentines. Most of them were in red envelopes — homemade red envelopes. There were at least twenty-five!

And on the back of each envelope was a skull and crossbones.

Angela had a feeling that these were not run-of-the-mill Valentines. She didn't think they were funny Valentines either. She opened one and looked at it. It was a pop-up card. For a moment Angela was very impressed. Luther had made it himself, and a lot of work had gone into it. There was a picture of a baboon in a cage, and the cage popped up. The baboon was wearing a shirt that said, "ANGELA."

In another envelope there was a red finger-painting of a heart with an arrow through it. "POISON ARROW FOR ANGELA," it said.

Angela decided not to open the rest. Luther had probably sent her the meanest Valentines in history.

She glanced through the other Valentines. The one from Cheryl said, "MY SPECIAL FRIEND." Angela wondered if she had sent the same one to everyone in the class. There was also a white envelope from Miss Berry.

Angela was not surprised that her kindergarten teacher had sent her a Valentine. But inside that envelope there was another one. It was a card with hearts on it. She opened it.

Guess who?

Angela recognized Eddie's handwriting immediately.

She looked in the other envelope and read the note from Miss Berry.

Dear Angela,

This came in the mail for you along with a nice letter from Eddie's grandmother. They are all living with Eddie's father now, who has a job in Seattle. It sounds like a good job, and Eddie is happy at his new school.

I just wish she had remembered to put their return address...

Angela stuffed all the Valentines into her book bag and turned around. Luther was watching her.

He was waiting for her to say something.

Angela thought about all the work he had done, so she said, "Thank you for all the Valentines. They were . . . um . . . very insulting."

Luther seemed pleased. "Which one insulted you the most?" he wanted to know.

"I'll have to read them over . . . more carefully," Angela said. "I'll let you know on Monday," she promised.

Luther nodded.

Cheryl grabbed Angela in the hallway.

"I just so happen to know that those red ones are private Valentines," Cheryl said. "Luther gave all his Valentines to you, but I'm not telling Miss Blizzard." She leaned closer and said, "And do you know why?"

Angela just stared at Cheryl.

"Because I think you and Luther make a good couple," Cheryl said, "because Luther likes you."

"Luther hates me," Angela said. "Those were mean Valentines. He's always mean to me."

Cheryl laughed very loudly. "Angela, don't you know anything? That's how you know when a boy likes you. He has to be mean to you first!"

Angela felt confused, but she didn't have time

to think about romance right now; she had a tight schedule.

As soon as she got home she got the keys and went up to say hello to Moxie and to tell her she would be back at 6:32 to feed her dinner. She came home exactly at four o'clock and changed into her party dress. As she was taking her schedule out of her book bag, she saw all the red envelopes — the Valentines from Luther.

Angela sat down at her desk and thought for a moment. She took out her Wedding Diary.

Eddie had asked her first, so she couldn't marry Luther. But maybe Luther could be Best Man. . . .

She read over what she had written:

Flower girl= Mandy
Mother of the bride=
              Mommy
Brides maid= Tina
Matron of honor-
       Mandy's sister
       (Find out name)
Best man=Nathaniel

Angela crossed out Nathaniel and wrote in "Luther" after BEST MAN.

Now what would she do about Nathaniel? She wanted him to be very important at her wedding.

She drew a map of the deck of the ferry and made a mark where each member of the wedding party would stand.

She suddenly got a brilliant idea. Her father *and* her brother would give her away.

"Me, Nathaniel, and Daddy hold hands and waltz up ile," she wrote.

Angela was against marching at a wedding. She felt it was too military. She had decided the waltz was the most beautiful dance in the world. For the music she already had chosen her favorite waltz — a cowboy song called *Rye Whiskey*.

Angela read quickly over the marriage vows as she had remembered them from her Aunt Patty's wedding.

Captain of Ferry:
"Dearly beloved,
We are gathered
here today to join this
man and this woman in
bonds of deadly wedlock

She read right to the end when the Captain finally says, "I now denounce you man and wife."

But the Captain would not say, "You may now

kiss the bride." Not at Angela's wedding.

She and Eddie would shake hands. Angela had nothing against kissing, as long as it wasn't on the lips, but she thought a handshake was a more appropriate way to seal the marriage vows.

Angela looked at her watch. It was twenty-five minutes after four. Mandy would be here in five minutes!

Chapter XVI

The Great Waldo Bows Out

Mandy was late. At four-thirty Angela heard Tina complaining that Nathaniel was in the shower.

"He's been in since he got home from school. I have to wash my hair, too. I have ballroom dancing. I have to be ready at five-thirty."

At a quarter to five Nathaniel was still in the shower. Tina was furious.

"Do something, Mom!" she wailed.

Tina's mother was in the kitchen frying chicken for the birthday dinner, and couldn't leave the stove. "Nathaniel!" she called.

Nathaniel let Tina take a shower, but as soon

as she got out, he got back in.

At five o'clock her father left for a concert rehearsal. Mandy still hadn't arrived.

Angela tried to think of a nice way of telling Mandy that even if she came late, she would have to leave at six-thirty, no matter what. Angela had promised Moxie to be back at 6:32.

Just then the doorbell rang. "I can't leave the stove," Angela's mother called.

Angela answered the door. It was Mandy and her sister. Mandy looked very nice in a red skirt and colorful sweater with big Valentines all over it.

"Would you like to come in?" Angela asked Mandy's sister.

"I'll have to." Mandy's sister smiled. "I have your presents in my bag." She set her shoulder bag on the front hall table and emptied everything out. There were three birthday presents for Angela in the bag. "One from Mandy, one from me, and one from Phoebe. Phoebe sends her regrets," Mandy's sister told her.

Angela was praying that Nathaniel would finish his shower, get dressed in a hurry, and come out. She opened the presents as slowly as possible.

Mandy's present was a tiny cactus in a pot. Phoebe had sent Angela a "signed" photograph of herself — a picture of her with a muddy paw print at the bottom. "And this one's from me," Mandy's sister said, "but I didn't have time to write a card."

Angela opened the present. It was a copy of *The Wizard of Oz!* "Oh, thank you," she said. "Thank you!"

Mandy's sister whispered, "Mandy told me how Miss Blizzard took the book away from you, and the story made me sick."

Angela hugged the book and stared up at Mandy's sister. She thought she was the loveliest person she had ever seen.

"Can you stay for the party?" she whispered.

Mandy's sister laughed and shook her head. She began repacking her shoulder bag.

"Could you wait just a minute?" Angela begged her. The water in the shower was no longer running.

She turned and ran down the hall.

Nathaniel was in his room blow-drying his hair. He had a towel wrapped around him.

"Please hurry up and get dressed so you can meet Mandy's sister," Angela said. "She's standing in our hallway right this minute . . . and Nathaniel," she whispered, "she's very beautiful."

"In a minute. In a minute," Nathaniel said.

Angela tried to be patient.

Finally she went back to the hall, but Mandy's sister was gone.

"She had to leave," Mandy told her. "She has a date. This guy she likes finally asked her out."

Angela was sorry to hear that.

She looked at her watch. It was a quarter after five. The Magic Show was supposed to have started fifteen minutes ago. She went to get Nathaniel.

Nathaniel still had the towel wrapped around him. He was in his parents' bedroom talking on the telephone to Doug. Nathaniel was writing things down.

"More ideas. More ideas," he kept saying. "What do I talk about after that?"

Doug was giving Nathaniel ideas of what to talk about to Lola!

"Nathaniel," Angela whispered. "What about The Great Waldo?"

Nathaniel turned to look at her.

"Who?" he asked.

"Great Waldo the Magician," Angela said. "Your magic act!"

Nathaniel said thoughtfully, "That's not a bad idea. But only if I get desperate for material. I'm not sure Lola would think it was all that funny."

Angela gave up.

The Great Waldo did not make his appearance, so Angela read *The Wizard of Oz* out loud to Mandy while Mandy read over her shoulder. Her mother brought in a checkered tablecloth, and they had an "inside picnic" on the living room floor. "The kitchen got too smoky," her mother explained.

Mandy seemed to be having a very nice time.

To Angela's relief, Nathaniel left for the theater ten minutes early. He looked very handsome in his new jeans and sweater. But then he had to come back three times. Once, because he forgot his wallet. Once for his keys, and the third time because he forgot something else, but he couldn't remember what it was!

Mandy's mother was late. She didn't pick Mandy up until seven o'clock.

Then the two mothers chatted in the doorway. Fifteen minutes went by. Angela felt desperate.

She was going to be forty-five minutes late for Moxie! Finally Mandy's mother and her mother said good-bye.

The telephone rang. Angela went to answer it.

"Did Lola call?" Nathaniel was calling from a public phone. He sounded out of breath. "She's not here yet. I'm standing in the lobby and the movie's already started."

"No. She didn't call," Angela said.

"Was anyone on the phone?" Nathaniel wanted to know. "Maybe she was trying to reach me and the line was busy."

"No one was on the phone," Angela said.

"Look," Nathaniel said. "Go in my room and get my address book. Her number is under 'L' for Lola. I want to make sure I'm calling the right number. There's no answer."

Angela went and got the address book. She went back to the phone and read it off to Nathaniel.

"That's the number I've been calling." Nathaniel's voice was breaking. "Angela," he said, "I'm standing here with two tickets and two popcorns and two sodas and . . ." He couldn't go on. He was crying.

"Don't cry, Nathaniel," she whispered.

"So, I was wondering what I should do," Nathaniel paused. Then he said, "Would you like to meet me here and see the movie?"

Angela didn't really care about seeing *Revolt of the Main Frames,* but she wanted to be with her brother. She didn't know how to cure a broken heart, but she had to try.

"I'll go ask Mommy," Angela said.

Angela ran into the front hall.

"Mommy, Nathaniel's on the phone. Lola isn't there."

"Oh, dear." Her mother looked very sad.

"Nathaniel wants me to go to the movie with him."

Her mother looked doubtful. "Well, I don't know about that movie. . . ."

"Mommy," Angela whispered, "he's crying."

"Poor Nathaniel," her mother said softly. She sighed. "Come on. I'll take you."

Angela went back to the phone and told Nathaniel she'd be right there.

She put on her coat and boots.

Then she remembered. "Moxie!" Angela said. "I have to feed Moxie."

"Well, that will only take a few minutes," her mother said.

Angela was shocked. She was planning to spend at least an hour and a half with Moxie. She decided she would make it up to Moxie tomorrow.

Angela went to the front table to get the keys. The keys weren't there.

Chapter XVII

Fairy Tale

Angela and her mother searched all over for the keys. "I know I put them on the table," Angela said.

"I'll bet Nathaniel took them by mistake. He was in such a hurry. Come on, Angela," her mother said. "We'll go to the movie theater and get the keys from Nathaniel. Then I'll come home and feed Moxie. You stay with your brother and watch the movie. You're the only one in the family who seems to be able to comfort Nathaniel."

Angela felt good to hear that.

When they got down to the lobby, Angela's mother asked the doorman if there was a second set of keys for Tony and Pamela's apartment.

"I'm afraid not," the doorman said.

"What if Nathaniel doesn't have them?" Angela asked her mother. "Can we break down the door?"

"I hope it doesn't come to that," her mother said.

Angela suddenly blinked her eyes. Mandy's sister was walking into their lobby. She was holding Moxie's keys. She handed them to Angela.

"I'm sorry, I picked these up by mistake. I have exactly the same key chain."

Angela took the keys and held them tight. She looked up at Mandy's sister.

Angela was sure Mandy's sister had been crying. Her eyes were red.

"Her parents probably gave away Phoebe," she thought. Angela felt embarrassed for her. She looked down and found herself staring at the pretty butterfly ring Mandy's sister always wore on her finger.

"Is Phoebe all right?" she mumbled.

"Oh, Phoebe's fine." Mandy's sister turned to Angela's mother and said, "Please excuse my appearance, but I was waiting at a movie theater and my date never showed up. Then I found out that *The Revolt of the Main Frames* was playing at four different movie houses, and he never told me which one, so I thought I'd just drop these by . . . um . . . on the way home."

"Are you Mandy's sister?" Angela's mother asked.

"Oh, I'm sorry. I meant to introduce myself. We didn't get a chance to meet before. I'm Mandy's sister. I'm Lola."

That night Angela told Moxie a true fairy tale.

"And so, Moxie," she concluded, *"Mandy's sister turned out to be the same Lola — The Real Lola. The Beautiful Lola. Nathaniel had forgotten to tell her which theater to meet him at, and they went to different theaters. My mother and I took Lola to meet Nathaniel, and Nathaniel was very happy."*

Angela took a deep breath. "Lola and Nathaniel begged me to stay to watch the movie with them, but I told them I couldn't. Moxie was waiting for me."

Moxie purred.

"There had been a lot of suffering," Angela went on, *"but the story has a happy ending. For it appears that, ever since the first day of school, Nathaniel and Lola*

secretly liked each other, but little did they know, they liked each other back. Nathaniel and Lola were attracted to each other."

Moxie nudged Angela's shoulder. Angela turned and looked at the black cat. " 'Attracted to each other' means . . . um . . . they were both under a spell," she explained.

Moxie seemed satisfied with that definition, so Angela continued, "And so it seems they are going to have a relationship."

Moxie jumped to her feet and began to flick her tail.

Angela studied Moxie. "Oh, I see what you mean. Well, I guess 'going to have a relationship' means they will probably live happily ever after," Angela explained. Moxie curled up on Angela's lap again, closed her eyes, and began to purr.

It was getting late. Angela showed Moxie a few steps in a new dance Tina was teaching her called the rhumba and kissed her good-night.

"I'll read you some of The Wizard of Oz tomorrow," Angela promised.